KU-022-996

CONTENTS

THE BODY
in the
DUMB RIVER

GEORGE BELLAIRS

with an introduction by
MARTIN EDWARDS

This edition published 2019 by
The British Library
96 Euston Road
London NW1 2DB

The Body in the Dumb River was originally published
in 1961 by John Gifford, London

The Body in the Dumb River © 1961 George Bellairs
Introduction © 2019 Martin Edwards

Cataloguing in Publication Data

A catalogue record for this book is available from the British Library

ISBN 978 0 7123 5214 7
eISBN 978 0 7123 6480 5

Front cover image © NRM / Pictorial Collection /
Science & Society Picture Library

Typeset by Tetragon, London
Printed in England by CPI Group (UK) Ltd, Croydon, CRO 4YY

THE BODY
in the
DUMB RIVER

INTRODUCTION

The Body in the Dumb River, also published under the title *Murder Masquerade*, first appeared in 1961, twenty years after its author's first novel. At that point in his career, George Bellairs had established a solid reputation as a crime writer, and would soon be able to retire to from his day job as a Mancunian bank manager to the Isle of Man, where he happily concentrated on his fiction.

The story is very much in the traditional vein. Bellairs' series detective, Tom Littlejohn (by this stage elevated to the rank of Superintendent), is visiting the fen country of East Anglia when he is asked to take a hand in a murder investigation. It soon emerges that the deceased, Jim Lane, was leading a double life. His real name was James Teasdale, and he had a wife and family back in Yorkshire whom he'd kept in the dark about his working on a fairground, and about the woman he lived with, Martha Gomm. Littlejohn's enquiries lead him to Yorkshire, and he sets about unravelling the mystery of Teasdale's fate with his customary blend of shrewdness and compassion.

George Bellairs was the pen-name of Harold Blundell (1902–82), who combined a long career in provincial banking with an equally hard-working life as author of no fewer than fifty-eight detective novels. His debut, *Littlejohn on Leave*, is now exceptionally rare; it was written to while away the time while Blundell was serving as an air-raid warden, having been excused military service because he was blind in one eye.

Bellairs was evidently a man to whom loyalty came as second nature. He started working for Martins Bank at the age of fifteen, and remained with the same institution until he retired, having reached the position of head office manager in Manchester, in 1962; seven years later, Martins was taken over by Barclays. Similarly, he stayed with the same publishers (John Gifford, and their alter ego the Thriller Book Club) all his life, although as the late R.F. Stewart explained in a witty article, 'The Very Faithful Servant' (CADS 24, November 1994), the unattractive payment terms he received meant he was never in a position to give up the day job prematurely.

Stewart's essay remains to this day the most entertaining survey of Bellairs' life and work. He mentions, for instance, that in 1945 Bellairs gave a talk about crime fiction to his local Rotary Club in Rochdale, arguing that detective stories flourished in democracies but not dictatorships – only for one of his superiors at the bank to write a condescending note saying: 'I have read with great interest the cutting from the *Rochdale Observer*... You produced a very interesting point of view and, while I hope and believe I am a good democrat, I must say that seven-eighths of the crime fiction I have come across is as unwelcome to me as the dictators'.

Undeterred, Bellairs continued to give talks, as well as writing a regular travel column for the *Manchester Guardian*. For *Martins Bank Magazine*, he contributed a characteristically light-hearted article, 'Sherlock Holmes and the Bankers', to celebrate the great detective's alleged hundredth birthday in 1954. He argued that Lloyds Bank, which took over Cox & Co in 1923, 'also presumably absorbed as well' Dr Watson's battered tin dispatch-box containing all his records of Sherlock's cases; he concluded with an appeal to Lloyds to 'investigate the case of the missing records and let us know the truth about them without delay'. In addition to his literary and banking work, Bellairs was also a diligent committee man, not least on behalf of the Manchester Royal Infirmary. His efforts on behalf of local causes, coupled with his crime writing, led to Manchester University conferring an honorary M.A. upon him in 1959.

In the following year, Bellairs consulted his friend Francis Iles (who had reviewed several of his books with considerable generosity) about his publishing contracts. Iles was a pen-name of Anthony Berkeley Cox, who as Anthony Berkeley had been a highly successful Golden Age detective novelist, whose successes included *The Poisoned Chocolates Case*, also an entry in the British Library's Crime Classics series. Under the Iles name, he was a pioneer of the psychological crime novel with an ironic twist, but he had given up writing fiction to focus on reviewing. A man of strong opinions, he was appalled by the way Bellairs was being treated, and advised him to re-negotiate his terms with John Gifford, saying: 'Oh, my poor fellow!... This is an utterly iniquitous contract. In fact it's the worst I've ever seen.'

Bellairs was evidently as meek and mild-mannered as Berkeley's character Ambrose Chitterwick, but he duly raised the matter with his publishers, only to be rebuffed ('this would be contrary to general practice and a precedent fraught with danger') and told, implausibly, that they had never even heard of the Society of Authors. This brutal response seems to have been enough to intimidate him into acquiescence; perhaps he lacked the self-confidence to take up Iles' robust advice to try his luck elsewhere. Stewart, having examined Bellairs' archive, which is held at the John Rylands Library in Manchester, concluded that the author's net income from hardback publications in the UK was negligible, although he did sell in the USA until the early Fifties, and overseas, especially in France: 'the money from his books was a bonus, and he was honest enough to admit it. He was an amateur enjoying a paying hobby.'

This is a fair summary, and by no means an ignoble epitaph. Yet one should not under-estimate the achievement of publishing so many books over a period of about four decades. Bellairs may not belong in the front rank of crime novelists, but his books offer unpretentious entertainment, and that has enduring worth. So much so, in fact, that following the British Library's republication of three of Bellairs' early mysteries in the Crime Classics series, sales were extremely healthy and the response from readers and reviewers highly enthusiastic. And the welcome result is a continuation of the George Bellairs revival with the reprinting of this title and also of *Surfeit of Suspects*.

Martin Edwards

www.martinedwardsbooks.com

THE BODY IN THE DUMB RIVER

'Are you awake, Littlejohn?'

'Yes. What is it?'

The first knock had roused him, but Littlejohn hadn't quite remembered where he was and answered in the brusque tone of one dragged from a comfortable night's sleep. Then his mind clicked broad awake and he realised that he was the guest of the Chief Constable of Fenshire.

'Is that you, Sir Humphrey?'

'Yes. Mind if I come in?'

'Not at all.'

It had been one of those cases where Scotland Yard had co-operated at the London end of a forgery affair which had started in Ely, and Littlejohn had been at the Fenshire police headquarters helping to tidy up matters for the next assize. It had rained without cease for a week before his arrival and it had continued through the whole visit.

The Chief Constable, a charming man, had invited Littlejohn to dine at his home and after doing him the full honours of his table and his cellar, had insisted on his staying the night, as the rain was still coming down in torrents.

Littlejohn's host, a tall, military type, now stood at his bedside, very apologetic and very worried-looking.

'Sorry to spoil our hospitality in this way, Superintendent, but I know you wouldn't like me to leave you in bed when we've a murder on our hands.'

He was wearing gumboots and a raincoat and said he hadn't yet been to bed.

Littlejohn glanced at his watch on the bedside table.

Three o'clock. Outside he could hear the steady beat of the rain on the trees and the lawn, now strewn with the dead leaves of late October.

'Just as I was about to turn in, news arrived that the River Lark had burst its banks between Ely and Feltwell and flooded the village of Tylecote. We've been arranging the rescue teams and relief work and now, right in the middle of it all, a showman has been found stabbed in the back. If this downpour continues, we'll be extended to the full here, with very little time even for a murder case. I hope you don't mind if I ask Scotland Yard to lend you to us for a day or two.'

'I don't mind a bit, sir. When you telephone them, please ask them to send my colleague Sergeant Cromwell down, too...'

He hastily dressed himself and, as he did so, the Chief Constable filled in some details.

'Since before records were kept, there's been an annual hiring-fair at Tylecote-in-the-Fen, between Ely and Feltwell. Once, it was the occasion for recruiting farm labourers; now it's degenerated into a spree of roundabouts, sideshows, coconuts and shooting-ranges. It's due to be held in a couple of days. This year, it will be a complete washout; the showground's a bog already.'

The pair of them made for the dining-room where coffee was ready.

'The murdered man, James Lane, ran a sideshow at the fair. He's been a regular attender for several years, they tell me. A harmless little fellow by all accounts. His body was found sprawling across a broken tree trunk which the floods had brought down and got jammed at Tylecote Bridge. They say it looks as if someone had thrown him in the Dumb River after he died, hoping to get rid of

him. The flood water must have dislodged the body and brought it
to light before the murderer intended.'

'The Dumb River...?'

'I suppose it got the name because, in quiet times, it flows without a sound. Tonight it's making noise enough. It's really a drain
these days, constructed more than a century ago by deepening and
widening an existing brook. Normally, it would be a good place for
getting rid of a corpse. The water's dark and muddy-looking and
there's little flow in it. Cast a dead body among the reeds and mud
there and it might never be found.'

'I'm ready, sir.'

'We've about twelve miles to go.'

As they made their way, the whole countryside seemed alive.
Lights dotted the farmland of the fens like a swarm of fireflies.
Houses all lit up, car headlamps and torches shining everywhere.
Now and then a car or a lorry swished past, casting feathers of
water on either side. Sometimes a shadowy figure, leaning forward
against the wind. All in a hurry. No time to stop and greet anyone
or indulge in futile talk about the weather. Everything available was
converging on the distressed areas.

The wipers of the Chief Constable's car flashed to and fro, and
here and there, where the road ran beside the river, they could see
the tormented water tearing along, bearing on its way anything
loose it could pick up. The sky was obscured by low clouds, the air
was damp and cold, and the beams of the headlights illuminated
the rain, pelting down in slanting shafts like the hatching of an
engraving.

Tylecote was little more than a hamlet standing by the bridge
where the Dumb River joined the Lark. There were a few houses
scattered about, most of them showing lights, a shop, a pub, and a
church with a massive tower tucked among some trees.

'The body's at the Blandish Arms, and here we are.'

A low, rambling building with outhouses and illuminated in almost every room. A few cars spread about the roadside, and an ambulance. A squad of policemen and firemen standing around drinking tea. They all straightened and some of them saluted when the two men entered.

The landlord was limping here and there, anxiously doing his best to provide hospitality. It was an out-of-date place, with two public rooms, the larger of them stone-floored and sanded. A bar, leather-upholstered benches, and small tables scattered about. The usual pumps and bottles on the counter, a dartboard in one corner, advertisements for beer tacked on the walls, and a large old-fashioned grate with a dying fire shedding its ashes over the hearth.

A tall, burly countryman in the uniform of a police inspector met the newcomers at the door.

'This is Inspector Diss, Littlejohn.'

'We were together this afternoon, sir. I didn't expect we'd meet again at this hour on a night like this, Diss.'

'I've arranged with Scotland Yard for the Superintendent to stay with us till the murder case is solved.'

'Delighted to hear it, sir. We'll need all the men we can get. The river's over its banks by nearly four inches in Hook's Hollow just down the road and if this rain keeps up, we'll have to start thinking about evacuating the ground floors of some of the cottages. You remember what happened last time...'

There was a stir of curiosity and satisfaction among the onlookers. Scotland Yard's on the job, so we're all right! One or two of them introduced themselves to Littlejohn, wrung his hand, and thanked him profusely. He might have solved the crime already!

The limping landlord was still bustling about. He, too, shook hands with Littlejohn as though he'd known him all his life.

'The body's in the brewhouse. We don't brew there now. So, it's all right, isn't it? The doctors are there, too.'

Men in waders kept wobbling in, drinking hot tea, and then vanishing in the dark. There seemed to be some schedule about the rescue work, but Littlejohn couldn't make out the pattern of it.

'Like to see the body?'

The landlord, a little bald man with a club-foot and in his shirt-sleeves, was disappointed. This chap didn't seem interested. He thought famous detectives always saw the body right away. Littlejohn was busy talking to the two men who found it, as if that would do any good.

Two labourers, answering a civil defence call, had seen the body first.

'As we passed the old ford, near where the Dumb River joins the Lark, we see this tree-trunk catched up among a lot o' rubbish the water was bringin' down. Didn't we, Joel?'

Joel, a simple-Simon of a fellow, who seemed as dumb as the river, smiled and exposed a gap where some teeth had once been. He nodded.

'Ar.'

His companion was different. He had a hatchet face, dark gipsy eyes bright with curiosity and excitement, and he wore three days' growth of swarthy whiskers.

'Just as we passed it, the dead man's head sort of appeared round the tree-trunk, peepin' at us, like. Like a turnip, it looked. Matter o' fact, I sez to Joel, that's a funny turnip, that is. And then we see what it was. Gave us both a proper turn. Didn't it, Joel?'

Joel looked proud of the turn and nodded joyfully.

'Ar.'

'So you got down and pulled the body out, Trimmer?'

'We did that. He might not 'a been dead, you see, sir. But he was. Not that we knew that he'd been murdered till we got here at the Arms and Clifton spotted it right away.'

The Chief Constable glanced around the room.

'Where is Clifton?'

Clifton was the village bobby, now, to his great delight, living with his wife and four children in a new police house.

'He's gone off to bring his grandmother to the police station. She lives in Hook's Hollow, sir, and there's four inches of water in her livin'-room. She's turned ninety and Clifton said…'

'What about the body, sir? Forgotten it?'

The landlord was getting peevish about the neglect of his exhibit.

'Yes, the body. Where is it?'

'I said in the brewhouse, sir, and we don't brew there any more, since the brewery took us over.'

'Lead the way, then, Goodchild.'

Diss, who joined them, offered Littlejohn a cigarette with a smile.

'I always like a smoke when I've to inspect anything in the morgue.'

He took one himself from a tin in his pocket.

'My home-made ones are far better and I keep 'em in a separate tin. I can't offer you one, sir, because I've licked 'em to make them stick.'

The brewhouse was a square stone appendage and there were lights on inside. The landlord pompously led the way, but when he saw what was going on, he hurried back to the bar and consumed a large brandy.

Two men turned to greet them. The building had been cleaned up and tidied. Along one wall, a couple of old-fashioned vats had been left from the days when they made home brew there, and a large porcelain sink which had obviously just been in use. Whitewashed walls and a stone floor. Overhead, a large electric bulb threw a dazzling light on the trestle table beneath it. The body of the dead man was lying on the table covered by a sheet.

Both doctors had washed and changed after their examination and were smoking cigarettes. One of them, the police surgeon, was elderly and squat, with a mop of unruly white hair and a healthy pink face. The other, a pathologist, was in formal black jacket and grey trousers, dark and sleek-haired. He looked like a corpse himself.

They all shook hands.

The elder of the two apologised for what might have seemed undue haste in getting down to work.

'When it was reported by the coroner's officer, I said we'd better get on with the job right away. So, I got Harkness up and we made a start. If this rain persists and there's widespread flooding in the district, travel from place to place will be difficult. Besides, there'll be other work for doctors to be doing for the living, without dealing with the dead.'

The attendant policemen were packing the doctors' bags and whispering together in a corner, as though the funeral had begun already. The younger doctor was obviously eager to be getting away. He couldn't keep still. He walked up and down as though anxiously waiting for someone, and now and then nervously rubbed his palms together. The elder was more composed. He acted as spokesman.

'A stab in the back. Might have been done with a butcher's knife or something similar. It passed through the heart. Quite a healthy man, though not used to hard work. Nor, I'd think, capable of much physical endurance. I'd guess he was attacked; there are bruises on the body which indicate rough handling. Of course, the debris in the water might have caused some abrasions and contusions, but we both think that, apart from that, he'd had a rough-house from someone. The bruises were, in our view, inflicted whilst he was alive. It's a bit difficult to be precise about the time he died on account of his immersion in the river. He'd eaten a meal of corned beef and tomatoes not long before his death. Probably some time Sunday night or early Monday morning. He was dead when he reached the water. The state of the lungs proves that.'

Harkness was getting anxious. He put on his hat and raincoat and struggled into his gumboots.

'I really must be going.'

He sounded like a castaway eager to get back to civilisation.

'I want some sleep. If this damned rain keeps it up, we'll have a few sleepless nights before we've finished.'

'Take a look at the body, then, Superintendent. As Harkness says, we'd better be off.'

The body was naked. The *tête-à-tête* between Littlejohn and James Lane was very brief. The Superintendent was aware of the sutured incisions without even looking at them. There was a patch of plaster here and there and neat livid lines where the scalpels had cut their way and the needles neatly finished it.

The victim was not as large as Littlejohn had imagined. Not the fairground type at all. A little man, lightly built, white-fleshed, small-boned. More like a clerk or a modest shopkeeper. Bony, too. Almost undernourished and flat-chested.

The eyes were closed. The hair was fair, turning grey over the temples. It had been closely cut and was strong and bristling. A good forehead and a large nose with a narrow, firm chin. The pale lips were thin and the mouth wide.

Littlejohn gently replaced the sheet. By some strange flight of imagination, he imagined Lane's companions of the fairground calling him 'Little Jim'.

The doctors left them and they could hear them splashing across the courtyard and then shunting their cars about and driving off.

'Did Lane wear spectacles, Diss?'

Diss raised his eyebrows.

'I noticed a red mark across the bridge of his nose.'

'Yes, he did. I remember last time I saw him on the fairground a year ago, he had them on. He took them off, too, to clean them, and his eyes were so deep-set, he looked a completely different chap without them. He peered about him, too, as though he were half-blind with them off. He must have had weak eyes, because he wore sunglasses clipped over his spectacles, although it wasn't sunny. He'd no glasses on when they brought the body in. If he had them knocked off in a fight, he'd be severely handicapped, I'm sure.'

'How was he dressed?'

'He was by way of being a bit of a dandy. We've put his things to dry in the pub. They were a sorry mess after being immersed in the river. But he had on the same suit he wore when I saw him here before. A kind of grey light-woollen cloth with a pretty loud check pattern. And he wore a soft shirt of the non-iron sort and a silk bow-tie. He'd a natty tweed hat on, too, as a rule. More like an artist than a fair-man. I'd say he was a cut above the average fairground johnny.'

'What was his line?'

'Rather a degrading catch-penny affair for a man of his type. A game called hoop-la. You throw rings over objects like cheap china ornaments, gimcrack jewellery, little dolls, and packets of chocolate. Sixpence a go, and the odds you land anything definitely against you.'

'He did well at it?'

'I guess he did. It was a one-man show and regularly appeared at all the fairs in the neighbourhood. All the lads of the village would have a bash at Little Jim's hoop-la when he was here. Some got fascinated and played for hours. Especially if they'd girls with them who took a fancy to some of the gaudy knick-knacks on the stall.'

'Where did he come from originally?'

'Yorkshire, judging from the address on his driving licence. A place called Basilden. His name wasn't Lane, either. It was James Teasdale.'

'Did he live in a caravan?'

'No, he took digs in the village. Here, he lodged regularly with Mrs. Southery in Mill Lane. We'll ask her in the morning whether he'd checked in with her before he died.'

'Are there any fairground people here now?'

'No. If some of the usual travelling toughs had been here, I'd have suspected some of them had been at Lane. He's had a nasty beating up from all accounts. But only three showmen arrived yesterday, and when they saw the state of the fairground, they cleared off right away.'

'Had Lane any family?'

'I don't know. We'll find out when we speak with the local police at Basilden.'

'What about identification?'

'I guess someone from his home town will come to see the body. Although there's a woman travels with him who'd do it, if she's still around. A decent girl, much younger than Lane. Name of Martha Gomm. She used to look after Jim's pitch when he took time off. She travelled as Martha Lane and I do believe Mrs. Southery thought they were married. They used to occupy the same room from all accounts.'

'Is she likely to be somewhere in the vicinity?'

'She'll not be far away, unless, of course, it's her who killed Lane. She's not the type, but you never know with women.'

They returned to the bar. The men they had left behind had gone and another rescue squad was standing around the fire, which had been made up. Men in waders, gumboots and waterproofs, drinking tea with rum in it. They looked to have been wallowing in mud and hurried off as soon as their drinks were finished.

'The cattle and sheep are knee deep in parts and if it keeps on like this, most of the ground floors of the houses in Tylecote will be under water,' said one of them before he splashed off to duty again.

A tall, flushed constable detached himself from the group and saluted the Chief.

'This is Clifton, our local constable, Superintendent...'

'Pleased to meet you, sir. Bit of a corker, this.'

He blew through his moustache heavily and, with one hand behind his back, pitched a half-smoked cigarette accurately in the fire.

'You got your grandmother to safety, Clifton?'

'Yes, sir. She didn't want to leave her cottage and said she'd far rather we put her to bed upstairs till it was all over. But I 'ad to insist. Now, she's tucked in, cosy and asleep, in the girls' room and the girls are up in the attics.'

Diss lit a cigarette and offered Littlejohn and Clifton one apiece from his public packet.

'Had Lane booked in at Mrs. Southery's this time, Clifton?'

'Yes, sir.'

'Was Martha Gomm with him?'

'Yes. She arrived Sunday morning to wait for him. As usual, he'd been up north for the week-end. He didn't put in an appearance, and Martha thought he'd been held up by the floods.'

'You called at Mrs. Southery's on your way back from seeing to your grandmother?'

'Yes. I just asked a question or two, but I didn't break the news about Lane being dead, Inspector. I thought that had better be done officially in the morning. Mrs. Southery's in enough trouble as it is, without Martha faintin' and havin' hysterics on her hands. The water's up to the front door. She was up when I called and the pair of them were carrying the furniture upstairs. I thought the time inopportune, to say the least. Was I right, sir?'

'Quite right, Clifton. It can wait. I hope you agree, Superintendent.'

'Certainly. There's little else we can do about Lane until morning. But Clifton might get on the telephone to the Basilden police and ask them if Lane had any connections there and, if so, notify them of his death. If he's a wife in Basilden, she'd better not come here. There's enough trouble about without her adding to it. Tell her the body will be sent north, if necessary, after the inquest. We'll probably have to make a journey there before this case is over.'

The landlord and his wife were still busy brewing tea and making sandwiches.

'Good job we'd laid in a lot of vittles for the fair,' Goodchild was saying. 'We'd have had all this left on our hands but for the rain. One door never closes but another opens…'

He had been drinking too much of his own rum and didn't quite know what he was talking about. Clifton gave him a withering look.

Outside, they could hear another car pulling up, driven by somebody in a hurry. A door slammed and a giant of a man, obviously a farmer, entered. He wore oilskins and rubber boots and shook himself like a great dog on the threshold.

The Chief Constable greeted him familiarly, for he was a J.P. of the county.

'Well, John. You seem like a man in a hurry.'

'Evenin', Humphrey. Sorry. Can't stay. My brother's lower fields are under water and it's a matter of getting his herd on higher ground, because God knows what it'll be like by morning if this rain keeps on, and the Lark bursts its banks down there. He 'phoned me for help. I'm taking a gang of men along in the van. I heard that you'd found a murdered man in the river. I called to tell you that there's a deserted car standing on the road between here and Leete, two miles from my place, just where the road approaches the Dumb River. Two of my men recognised the car as belonging to the dead chap, fellow called Lane, isn't it? Thought you might like to know.

Might find a clue in it, or something. And now I must be off. It's still coming down like hell...'

He swished out and they could hear him yelling to his men to get aboard again, and then the van roared away.

The Chief Constable turned to Clifton.

'Better have it towed to a safe place, Clifton. Take a man with you and mark out the spot where you find it with wooden pegs. It seems a waste of good men at a time like this to put them on guarding the car.'

The bobby hurried to the door and cast a grateful look over his shoulder. He left the room and could be heard talking to someone outside.

'You ought to be in bed. You'll get your death of cold. Go home till mornin', that's a good girl.'

But the good girl, whoever she was, took no heed. Instead, she pushed past him and entered the room. The light of the bare electric bulb fell on her streaming hair and her large dark troubled eyes glinted under it.

She looked at the group of men standing round the bar and then at the Chief Constable and his party by the fire.

'Mr. Lander just called to see if we were all right. He said James Lane has been found dead in the Dumb River. Is it true?'

She looked round the room again and there was a pause. As though each man were leaving the breaking of the news to someone else. Sir Humphrey took a step towards her, but she knew from the silence and the gentle gesture of sympathy the Chief Constable made with his hand as he approached her.

She seemed to freeze where she stood, uttered a great sob, turned, and went back into the darkness. The sound of her movements was silenced by the steady hissing of the rain and she departed like a ghost.

'Poor Martha Gomm,' said someone.

Littlejohn followed her out into the night and nobody went with him. They seemed to understand that this was his business and that he might wish to deal with it undisturbed.

2

MARTHA GOMM

TYLECOTE POLICE STATION STOOD ON HIGH GROUND AND THE water had not, as yet, invaded it. The door was open, emitting a shaft of light which shone across the flood water in the road and down the path through the constable's garden, through which a small stream was pouring to join the main deluge in the highway.

Martha Gomm was standing in the doorway, silhouetted against the brightness of the hall, waiting for Clifton to finish whatever business he had in hand and attend to her.

Littlejohn splashed his way over the road, the water almost up to the calves of his gumboots. When he reached her he took her by the arm and drew her inside.

'You'd better come in out of the rain, Miss Gomm. I'd like to talk to you.'

Inside, Clifton had finished ordering a vehicle to help him tow away the abandoned car at the scene of the crime.

'It's goin' to call here for me, sir, and I'll see the spot is marked out good and proper.'

'Have you rung up Basilden police yet, Clifton?'

'Yes, sir. They'll see the news is passed on. Then they'll ring us back.'

He looked a lot smaller without his helmet and cape, which hung dripping behind the door. In the room above, children were talking in high piping voices, excited by the stir at that late hour and a woman could be heard comforting them and telling them to get back to bed.

The room itself looked like the lost property office at a railway station. Jammed between the official desk, chairs, and files, with a coloured print of Her Majesty looking down on them from over the fireplace, were a formidable leather upholstered chair, two tin trunks, a small mahogany chest of drawers, a large framed photograph of an angry old man in whiskers, and a silver-plated teapot surrounded by a tea service. There was a gilded parrot cage on the constable's desk and the occupant sounded wide awake in spite of the cloth which covered it. He kept making noises like the popping of corks and the pouring out of drinks. Now and then he shouted, 'Jolly good health to you and me.'

Clifton thought he owed an explanation.

'The old lady's things, just put there tempr'y, sir. She wouldn't come without them and we 'ad to load them in the van with her to humour her. She'd have brought her bed, too, if we could have found room to get it in.'

Martha Gomm stood in the doorway of the room, seeming neither alarmed nor surprised at finding herself there. She had obviously been disturbed in rescue work of some kind, for she was wearing a blue duffle coat, riding breeches and rubber boots. Her head was bare and her dark straight hair fell almost to her shoulders.

'Did you wish to speak to me about James?'

The voice was deep and husky. She was of medium build and well made. Her mannish get-up was counterbalanced by a refined feminine face. She had a foreign look, perhaps due to gipsy blood. High cheekbones, pointed chin, ivory complexion, and a straight nose, rather too long for prettiness, but adding a touch of character to her features. Certainly no fairground wanton, but a woman who might have known better places.

She spoke without a smile or a greeting.

'What happened to him?'

'His body was found in the Dumb River, Miss Gomm. He'd been murdered.'

She didn't faint or make a scene. Her eyes just opened wider in puzzled horror and then she took a hold of herself.

'How…?'

'He'd been stabbed. When did you see him last?'

'He left for the north about three o'clock on Friday afternoon. We were at Midhurst then. I came here from Cambridge, where he dropped me on his way, and I caught a bus. I never saw him again. Why should anybody want to kill him?'

There was no excitement at all in the question. Only despair. She sounded like someone lost, but remained perfectly calm. Her large dark eyes were fixed on Littlejohn's face, fascinated. Violence, murder, distress might have been parts of her everyday existence and she had perhaps learned to take them as they came, half expecting them.

Clifton found chairs for them and then went in the back room and came back with cups of tea. Martha Gomm sat with her cup between her two palms, enjoying the comfort of the warmth.

'Do you think you could answer one or two questions? I'm sorry to press matters just now, but it is urgent.'

She nodded.

'Where have you been all day?'

'Since James left I've been with Mrs. Southery. She's afraid the flood will reach her house and cover the ground floor. We've been moving the furniture to the upper rooms. It took all day and then we went to help the woman next door. She's not well and can't lift her belongings.'

'You knew James Lane well?'

'Yes.'

'For how long?'

'Four years.'

'You've been together all that time?'

Another nod.

'How did you begin your life together?'

'We met at Tavistock Goose Fair a little more than four years ago. James never worked at week-ends and asked me to take charge of his pitch on Friday afternoon till he came back on Monday.'

'Four years ago?'

'Yes.'

'Do you know why he took the week-ends off, Miss Gomm?'

'Yes. He travelled north to see his family.'

She said it quite calmly and without any hesitation or excuses. It might have been a commonplace.

'How did you come to start travelling and living together?'

'My husband left me and James offered me a job. I helped him at the fairs.'

There was something about the way in which she called Lane 'James'. As though the familiar name of 'Jim', by which everyone else seemed to know and address him, were not respectful enough.

'Did your husband leave you because of James?'

'In a way…'

She was not being evasive. Only trying to find words to explain the situation properly.

'In what way did Lane cause you and your husband to break up?'

'Jack was beating me one day. He often did it when he'd had too much to drink. James intervened. There was a fight and Jack turned me out after that. The morning after, I found he'd gone. It was then that James offered me the job.'

'You then began to live together?'

'It was cheaper.'

Cheaper! Just that. No sentiment, no talk about falling in love, no excuses. It was cheaper to hire a room for the pair of them and live as man and wife.

'Have you seen your husband since?'

'He died a year later. I saw his body before they buried him.'

'How did he die?'

'He was at Shrewbury Fair with the roundabouts. He got drunk one night and walked into the Severn. He couldn't swim. They found death due to misadventure.'

'Were you and Lane at Shrewbury at the time?'

'No. We never went that far north. We were at Benenden in Kent when it happened. They sent out a police message for me over the wireless. I went to identify his body. He'd nobody else. The woman he lived with after me had left him and couldn't be found. They got my name and photo from Jack's papers.'

She gave all the answers in a slow, colourless voice, with a trace of accent from one of the midland counties, probably Oxfordshire. As question followed question, she seemed to grow sadder, as though the recent work in the floods had brought a measure of diversion which was now wearing off.

Clifton kept coming and going from room to room attending to the needs of rescue workers who arrived, drank tea, and took away bundles of blankets. They were too occupied with the work in hand to disturb Littlejohn and Martha Gomm.

'This fight. What happened?'

It might have been all irrelevant, a searching for useless details, but it was Littlejohn's way and Martha Gomm didn't seem to mind.

'As I said, Jack was beating me. He was drunk. James, who had his stall near our caravan, interfered and Jack knocked him down. I thought he'd killed James, but he got up and went for Jack again. He was only a small man and he'd no idea how to fight. Jack had been a boxer in his time. But James seemed to get in a terrible temper suddenly and flew at Jack's throat like a terrier. He took Jack by surprise, they fell, with James on top of Jack. Jack caught his head on the steps of the caravan and was unconscious when they picked him up. He was soon all right and I expected he'd seek out James and nearly murder him. Instead, he turned me out. Told me to go to James. He didn't even threaten what he'd do to him. I think he thought James was a bit mad. At any rate, he left with the show the next day and till he died, we never crossed his path again. I always thought it would have been worse if he hadn't taken a fancy at the time to a girl in a sideshow. She was a contortionist. They lived together till just before Jack's death.'

The grotesque, unequal fight between the little man and the bully, the comic finish, and the flight of Jack, reminded Littlejohn of Charlie Chaplin and of Mr. Polly and their husky enemies. Only Jack had got the idea that his rival was a madman, given him a wide berth, and run away with a spider-lady.

'Did you know anything about James Lane's private life or what he did before he became a fairground showman?'

'I never asked him. And he didn't talk much about it. He said he wished to keep his two lives apart.'

'How did he manage that?'

'I couldn't tell you. But he did manage it. His wife never seemed to guess what he did when he was away from home. He used to send her postcards every week from where we were, but I'm sure she'd no idea what he was doing there.'

'And you never tried to fathom what was happening at the other end of his life. At Basilden, was it?'

'Yes, Basilden.'

'Did he never talk to you about his wife and family?'

'Now and then. He had three daughters, he told me once when he was in the mood. He said he'd married above his station and his wife and daughters thought he was a failure. I'm sure he wasn't. I'm sure he was better than they were. He was out of place in the fairground life, but said it made plenty of money for him and he could keep his family the way they thought they ought to be kept.'

'Did he never hint to you what he did before he took up the fairground existence?'

'I think he kept an arts and crafts shop. He was a good artist. He sometimes used to draw scenes at the fair in black and white. They were very good. He did a portrait of me, too, once.'

It was bewildering. Littlejohn didn't know what to make of her. A woman whose beauty would have attracted many of the good types of the fairground, to say nothing of other places. She could have married some decent fellow and had a home of her own, settled and content, for the asking. Yet, she'd preferred the little, undersized James Lane, with nothing much to offer her except an irregular union and his protection, for what it was worth.

'Were you in love with each other?'

'Yes, if by that you mean that we understood one another and wanted to be together as much as we could.'

'And you were content to live together in the way you did?'

'Yes. He told me he didn't want to let his wife divorce him. He said it was because of the girls and the disgrace it might bring on his wife. I didn't mind.'

Few women had roused Littlejohn's curiosity as much as Martha Gomm. Unsmiling, calm, making not the least attempt to exert her feminine charms or look pretty. Her large hands were rough and soiled by hard work and her nose was a bit red from the chill of the night.

She must have been turned thirty and Lane was described as being in his early fifties. His clothes had suggested that he was a bit of a dandy. Perhaps they'd led a gay life together and, judging from her tranquility and slight air of distinction, they'd been good for one another, too.

'Had James Lane any enemies?'

Littlejohn had dropped into the way of calling him James, too, as though, by using the dead man's jaunty diminutive name, he might hurt Martha.

'None since Jack died, as far as I know. I don't think Jack hated him all that much. Jack was, as I said, living with another woman now and then, before he left me. His quarrel with James gave him the excuse he'd been wanting to go to her for good.'

'So you can't give us any idea of who might have killed him?'

'I've no idea. I keep trying to think.'

She passed her hand across her forehead in a confused way. It was obvious that the commotion caused by the flood had softened the blow of Lane's death for her. She hadn't realised what had happened yet. When things calmed down, then...

'When did you last see him?'

'He left me last Friday, as I said, for his usual week-end trip to Basilden. He was going by road in his car. He should have got back yesterday, after lunch. He said he'd travel through the night to get here quicker, because he'd heard over the wireless that there were floods in parts and he wanted to see if I was all right and if there would be a fair or not. He never turned up.'

'He should have left home on Sunday night, then.'

'That's right. Often, if the journey was a long one, he'd get back as late as Monday evening. I looked after the pitch if there was a fair on the Monday.'

She certainly wasn't at all like the usual murdered man's mistress they interviewed after a crime. She didn't put on an act, she didn't try to look bereaved and shocked, she didn't hesitate or stumble over her words. There was nothing pathetic about her, either. Looking straight at Littlejohn, dry-eyed, a little strained, she answered his questions clearly, asking no sympathy or pity.

'Why do you think Lane was murdered?'

For the first time, she flinched. It must have been the word murder. Whether she dearly loved this man so much older than herself, or just held him in respect and affection, she certainly didn't wish him that.

'I don't know. Perhaps it was blackmail.'

'Why?'

'I'm sure he comes from a place much better than a fair. As I said, he'd a family in the north and he told me they were a cut above him, to use his own words. For some reason, it seemed they despised him a bit. Why anybody should feel that way about James, I can't think. But it did strike me that he didn't want them to know how he got his money, in case it made them despise him more. After all, a fairground life can be a pretty low one. Suppose someone from the north found out and threatened to tell…'

'But that would be like killing the goose that laid the golden eggs.'

'I'm sure James wouldn't stand for anybody blackmailing him. I wonder if he got in one of his rages, like he did when Jack was beating me. He might have attacked the blackmailer like he did Jack, and the blackmailer might have defended himself instead of going unconscious like Jack did.'

'Yes. There's something in that. Did you ever get the impression that he was worried about something?'

'No. He seemed to enjoy the life. In fact, he once told me how happy he was to be free and with me, after the life he'd lived in the old days. I admit he must have had his troubles now and then. He used to talk to me sometimes about his family. His daughters were growing up. One, I think, was courting with a doctor. He seemed pleased about it when he heard. Another had taken up with a bookie and it upset him. But it didn't cause him sleepless nights. He just worried a bit, but always said it would come out all right.'

'His eyesight was bad, I believe.'

'Yes. He wore strong glasses. He'd had them since he was a boy.'

'With sunglasses over them?'

'Yes.'

'Summer and winter?'

'Yes.'

'Perhaps to hide his identity.'

'That could be so. He didn't want anybody to recognise him. He didn't want his family to know the life he led. It was natural he should wear them, feeling the way he did.'

'I wonder what his family thought he was doing when he was away from home.'

'They thought he was a commercial traveller. He told me. The family thought he worked for a firm called Oppenheimer and Company, suppliers of artists' materials and picture frames, in Manchester. He said, when I asked him, it was his alibi. He laughed about it. And he'd send his family a postcard regularly from the nearest big town where we travelled. I've posted them for him. Just to say he was well and trade was good and sending his love.'

'You know, of course, his real name wasn't Lane, but Teasdale?'

'Yes.'

'Did he ever tell you what attracted him to the fairground?'

'Yes. He owned a shop, as I said, in Basilden. He was by way of being an artist. He once told me that when he got married, he'd hoped to make his way in art, either by teaching or selling pictures. He'd won prizes for his painting and said he thought he might make a living in it. Well, it turned out to be a flop. So, he took a shop and dealt in arts and crafts – sold paints and things, and took photographs. He didn't do well even then and, as their family was growing, he looked out for something else. But he had no luck. Then, one day when there was a fair at Basilden, he found a show that was making a lot of money. It fascinated him, he said, because he saw behind the stall a whole bucketful of coppers that the man had made in profit.'

'So he started himself.'

'Yes, but not near home. He told his wife that some people he bought picture frames from had offered him a job on the road and, right up to his death, he pretended he was away on that, while all the time he was earning money on the fair.'

'By the bucketful?'

'No. The game James fancied and started was declared illegal almost as soon as he'd got going. So, he began taking photographs at fairs instead. That was a flop, too. Then, an old man and his wife who ran a hoop-la stall took him on as helper. He was on his uppers then and glad to take any job. The old man died and he bought the stall from the old lady. They were called Lane. Lane's Hoop-la. It was a well-known one at all the fairs and it did very well. You'd be surprised.'

Clifton was back and said they'd marked the spot where the car was found and towed it into the garage at the inn.

'There's nothin' particular in it. Inspector Diss is going over it now, but as far as I can see, it won't help us much. An old tumble-down thing it is, too.'

Footsteps splashed outside and then Diss arrived. He was carrying a battered fibre suitcase in one hand and over his arm, a suit of clothes.

'Hullo, sir. We found this suitcase in the boot of Lane's car. We were able to identify the car easily by the contents of the case. I

thought you'd like to see it, perhaps, and I brought across the suit
he was wearing, too, when we found him...'

He noticed Martha Gomm.

'Evenin', Miss Gomm. It's stopped raining, you'll be pleased to
hear.'

That explained the silence, the sudden lack of something, which
Littlejohn had noticed and wondered at.

'Could we just look through the contents of the suitcase? He
didn't leave it with you, then, Miss Gomm?'

'No. He usually took it in with him. He was always keen on having
clean linen and took his laundry home with him to be changed.'

She stood at Littlejohn's elbow as they turned out the contents
of the case. There was nothing to explain about it, or about the
pathetic crumpled check suit which Diss laid beside it on the table,
together with the foulard bowtie and the dead man's clean linen and
underclothes.

'That's his writing-case and diary...'

A cheap leather writing-case with damp notepaper in it, a few
picture postcards, already stamped, and some order sheets headed
Oppenheimer and Company, on which he'd probably listed fake
orders to show to his wife. There was a notebook, too, another cheap
little thing with nothing much in it, except a schedule of dates cover-
ing the fairs at which Lane was due to appear. They were roughly
south of a line from mid-Wales to the Wash, as though he gave his
hometown a wide berth. Nothing more. No names, no addresses.
Lane must have practised the utmost discretion in all he did, to
prevent his family obtaining the slightest inkling of the double life
he was leading.

Outside, the wind was rising and sweeping up the main road,
lashing the water lying everywhere into waves. It was just turned five.

'Hadn't you better go and get some sleep now, Miss Gomm?'

'If you don't need me any more.'

'We'll see you again tomorrow.'

'Good night.'

She left them without another word and they could hear her splashing her way home and then the sound of her died away.

A few people were still about outside, wading here and there, and now and then a vehicle passed, swishing water on each side. The floods would probably subside rapidly now that the rain had ceased and if there was no return of it, work would soon begin clearing up the mud and debris and drying everything out.

Another party of workers entered and drank tea in the back room. Clifton's family seemed to have settled down for the night and he hurried out to see to the needs of the firemen and constables who were asking for more blankets.

What to do next?

It was certainly a queer case. A man murdered. A little harmless sort of chap, with no enemies that anyone knew of, killed, and his body floating in the river with not a clue to guide them. Every trace of the crime washed away by the flood.

Diss took out an imitation leather binder from his raincoat pocket.

'I got this from Lane's jacket when we hung it up to dry, sir. They're bank statements bound together in a sort of wallet. We had to dry it page by page as it was soaked by the floods.'

The statements had been damaged by the water, but were plainly legible. They covered a period of five years, presumably since Lane had started his new life. The pass-sheets bore the name of a bank in Husband's Bosworth, Leicestershire, where perhaps Lane had attended his first fair.

The balance of the account had been small for the first year, but had then begun to rise very nicely. The present figure stood at two thousand pounds, built up in weekly payments, made at various banks on Lane's journeys from fair to fair. 'At Abchester', 'At Launceston', 'At Helston'... and so on.

There were no withdrawals, except one, made two days before Lane's death.

Diss looking over Littlejohn's shoulder, was fascinated by the figures.

'It's a life at which you can pocket and hide quite a lot of money. I'd like to bet that Lane didn't pay income tax on half he took at the fair. He never withdrew anything and that tells its own tale.'

'Except last week. Lane made his first withdrawal, then. He took out two hundred pounds. Could it be blackmail, Diss?'

Perhaps Martha Gomm had guessed right, after all.

3

WIFE AND FAMILY

T HE BEST WAY TO GET TO SHEFFIELD WAS BY THE HARWICH
boat train, which, they told Littlejohn, stopped at Ely just before
ten in the morning. A farmer took him to Ely to catch it. He was
half asleep. He'd spent two hours in bed at the inn in Tylecote and,
as he sat in the bouncing vehicle, he was too bemused to notice the
devastation on either side. He sat smoking his pipe, his hat on the
back of his head.

The road was under water part of the way. Sometimes it was
like fording a river with the flood up to the axles; at others, where
the torrent had broken the tarmac, streams crossed the road and
joined the overflowing ditches. On each side, huge lakes where once
the fields had been. In some of them, bewildered cattle stood knee-
deep, waiting to be rescued and in many of the trees on the wayside,
frightened hens were perching, looking down, wondering what to
do next.

Littlejohn had spoken to Cromwell, who hoped to arrive at
Tylecote about noon. He had given him instructions and left him to it.

The train reached Ely half an hour late and Littlejohn fell asleep
almost at once. He awoke half-way to Sheffield. The sun was shining
and there wasn't a trace of rain or floods. There was a dining-car
on the train and he lunched. At Sheffield, he had just time to catch
the local diesel. Basilden was a small manufacturing town on the
Yorkshire side of the Pennines.

At Basilden, he was the only traveller to descend from the train. It
was four o'clock and the sun was still shining. In spite of late October,

it was warm and dry. The ticket collector had a rose in the lapel of his coat. Littlejohn asked him the way.

'Teasdale? You mean the arty-crafty shop? Follow the road to the roundabout in the centre of the town. Then turn right. That's the main shopping street. High Street. The shop's just past the church on the left. You can't miss it. The name's over the window.'

Dusk was on the way and the sun was a dark copper colour. It added a touch of melancholy to the seedy street of shops leading to the town centre. In the distance, a range of low Pennine hills formed the background.

Littlejohn made the journey on foot. Grocers, butchers, little jewellers' shops selling knick-knacks instead of the real thing, sweets and tobacco, drapers, herbalists... All looked to be scratching for a living. Like James Teasdale had done before he took to the fair.

He followed the ticket collector's instructions, turned right at the cross-roads, and there it was. A large shop-window with a door on the right. The whole place needed a coat of paint. The window was untidily dressed with out-of-date pictures, reproductions, prints, with a Van Gogh looking out of place among the rest of the copies. The window-bottom was choc-a-bloc with paint-boxes, packets of drawing-pins, camel-hair brushes of all shapes and sizes, fretwork tackle, bookbinding leather. They looked as if they hadn't been disturbed for years. Over the window a large sign; faded gilt letters on a black background. J. TEASDALE. On one side of the name, ARTS AND CRAFTS; on the other, PHOTOGRAPHER.

Behind the glass panel of the shop door, rows of photographs had been fastened on a dark background with drawing-pins. They were studio portraits of men, women and children taken years ago, judging from their out-of-date style of dress. Some of them, improperly processed, had almost faded out. Martha Gomm had said James Lane hadn't made much of a success of photography. Littlejohn entered. Somewhere in the dim back quarters, a bell began to ring and continued until he found he hadn't properly closed the door. When he did so, the noise ceased.

He stood for a while in the shop. It was as if those in the rear premises were recovering from their surprise at the arrival of a customer and mustering courage to attend to him. The shop itself was cluttered up with more framed prints and on the counter were spread books of sample Christmas cards, presumably for orders for the coming season. The expanse of stuff packed in the window shut off most of the light and it was difficult making out the contents of the interior.

Suddenly, the door to the back quarters opened and a plump girl of about twenty-five emerged. She must have been washing her hair, for her head was swathed in a turban of towelling. Littlejohn could hardly make out anything but a buxom silhouette until she switched on a naked lightbulb, which illuminated the shop and exhibited its stark untidiness and air of defeat.

The girl was fair and blue-eyed, medium built and pretty in a heavy sort of way. She seemed a bit out of countenance on finding Littlejohn there.

'You must excuse me. I've just been washing my hair.'

She wasn't made-up but her complexion was good. There was a lazy look about her as though most things were too much trouble. She took up a position of salesmanship behind the counter.

'What can I do for you?'

'May I see Mrs. Teasdale, please?'

'What name is it?'

A voice from the room behind.

'Who is it, Barbara?'

And Mrs. Teasdale stood in the doorway, red-eyed with weeping, biting her lips to prevent another breakdown, a handkerchief rolled in a damp ball in one hand.

'My name's Littlejohn, madam. Superintendent Littlejohn. Could I speak with you in private?'

'Is it about my husband…?'

Her voice trembled. Littlejohn nodded. She stood aside and made a gesture with her head to invite him into the living quarters. Barbara scuttered ahead of them and hastily removed a large bucket from the hearthrug. Littlejohn never knew what it contained. Surely she hadn't been washing her hair in it!

Mrs. Teasedale was a woman of fifty-five or thereabouts. A plump type, fair hair turning grey, with a long face and a self-indulgent mouth and chin. She was dressed in a black silk gown, obviously in mourning already, but wore a pair of house slippers in which she shuffled about as though too lazy to pick up her feet. Her hair was slackly gathered in a bun at the back of her head.

Barbara had vanished. They could hear her in the room behind, rattling bottles and opening drawers, presumably finishing her toilet.

There were articles of sewing on the table. All black, as though the news had caused them to rummage among the crêpe and black braids of a workbox and start to stitch them together for a funeral. The furniture was old-fashioned and worn. On the wall above the fireplace, a dim picture of still-life, with initials J.T. in one corner. James Teasdale had won prizes for art. Littlejohn wondered if this were one of his *chefs-d'oeuvre*. He couldn't make head or tail of it. The colours were faded and dirty from the smoke which now and then puffed from the fire below it. On the opposite wall, above a cheap sideboard, a large photograph of a wedding group. It contained a complete family turn-out, from the looks of it. Forty or more people, in Sunday-go-to-meeting clothes, with the bridal pair in the middle front. Littlejohn recognised the younger version of the man he had last met on the mortuary table. The bride was hardly identifiable with the woman now sitting in the rocking-chair before him, slowly swinging to and fro, comforting herself from the motion. James Teasdale, in the picture, looked the meekest of the lot. It might have been a shotgun wedding!

On the cheap upright piano, with brass candlesticks screwed on its front, was a portrait of the Teasdale family. Mrs. Teasdale nursing a small baby, with a daughter on either side. It must have been a photograph by James himself, for he wasn't in it and the figures were slowly fading out in a halo of improper fixing.

'I gather the local police have passed the sad news on you, Mrs. Teasdale. I'm very sorry.'

'They said he had met with an accident and was dead. They told me that the part of the country where it happened was flooded and difficult to reach. They forbade me... yes, forbade me to go there and said you would be coming to tell me about the arrangements. Is it...?'

She spoke well, in an educated voice, and rolled the damp handkerchief in her hand, ready to use it if the occasion called for it. She seemed to be suffering more from shock – perhaps a sense of indignity, too – rather than grief.

'I will tell you anything you wish to know, madam, but I must ask you to be brave. Your husband was murdered at Tylecote yesterday.'

She stiffened and turned her terrified eyes on Littlejohn.

'Murdered? The police said it was an accident. They should have told me... Who did it? Have they made an arrest?'

'Not yet, Mrs. Teasdale. We are busy on the case at present.'

'Where is Tylecote?'

'In Fenshire.'

She relaxed.

'There's been some mistake. It can't be my husband. He had no business in Fenshire. In fact, we had from him this morning, posted in Nuneaton last Friday. He was travelling there for his firm.'

'I'm sorry, Mrs. Teasdale, but there's been no mistake. I have seen his body and I recognise him from the group on the wall there. Also, he carried a car licence bearing his name and this address. I wish it *had* been a mistake.'

'But what has happened? What was he doing in... where was it?'

'Tylecote.'

'Tylecote. Can you explain it all?'

'I know nothing, yet, Mrs. Teasdale. I happened to be there on another matter and, as the police are fully occupied with the floods, I offered to help them by coming to see you...'

She was on her feet, her grief forgotten, consumed by urgent curiosity.

'Barbara! Barbara!'

The girl appeared at the kitchen door. She seemed in no hurry. She wore a dressing-gown now and a blue net over her hair.

'Pack me a bag, Barbara. Your father's body is lying murdered in Tylecote and nobody there to look after him.'

'Don't be silly, Mother. You know...'

'It is true that your father has been murdered, Miss Teasdale, but you must persuade your mother to wait until his body is brought home. It is almost impossible for her to travel to Tylecote. There are extensive floods there and I can't promise she'll get there.'

'Murdered!'

Barbara looked ready to dissolve into hysterics and then her eyes fell on her mother, who was now busy rummaging in drawers, throwing things about, presumably packing for the journey.

'You heard what the man said, Mother. You can't get there. Besides, what are we going to do at a time like this with you on the other side of England?'

She seized all the things her mother had unearthed and rammed them back in the drawer. A brief scuffle occurred, as the two women tugged and snorted, one removing things from the drawer, the other thrusting them in again. Finally, Mrs. Teasdale broke into hard sobbing and flopped down in the rocking-chair.

'That's all the consideration I get in my trouble.'

'Never mind that, Mother. We'll have to get Irene and Christine home.'

Littlejohn had forgotten the other two girls, who, presumably had gone to work.

'Where are your sisters, Miss Teasdale?'

'Irene is a teacher; Christine is a receptionist at a dentist's. I'll just go next door and telephone for them. Excuse me.'

She put a coat over her *deshabille* and was off without another word.

Mrs. Teasdale sat gently rocking to and fro in the chair. Her eyes were fixed straight ahead, her hands still occupied with the sodden handkerchief.

'Do you feel able to answer one or two questions?'

'Yes. Will there be an inquest?'

'It will be held tomorrow at Ely, madam.'

'I must go to identify him. You see, it will be necessary for me to go, and I can bring his poor body home afterwards.'

She sobbed again and mopped her eyes slowly.

'Very well. You or one of your daughters will have to do that, but take it easy just now. Don't rush around and distress yourself. We will travel overnight and I can arrange for transport by the local police.'

'Barbara had better come with me. I can't bear it alone.'

'Your husband was away often?'

'Yes, he travels the southern counties as representative of Oppenheimer, of Manchester. A very responsible post. He is away all week and returns, as a rule, on Friday evening or Saturday morning, according to the distance he has to come. Then, he leaves on Sunday for his duties again. I can't believe...'

'He also ran his business here?'

'Barbara is in charge of it. People have lost the taste for art, for good pictures, nowadays, and my husband had not enough to keep him occupied in his own profession. So, he took another post to keep him busy.'

A different tale from the one Littlejohn had heard from Martha Gomm. He felt he daren't even mention Martha. The fat would be properly in the fire then and he didn't wish to be mixed up in any domestic scenes. In any event, probably the truth would be hotly denied, just as, at first, the murder and identity of the dead man had been.

'Why should anybody wish to kill my husband?'

She said it in a forlorn wail, shed more tears and mopped them off with the handkerchief again.

'He hadn't any enemies?'

'Certainly not. He was a peaceful man, who never quarrelled with anybody. A good husband, fond of his family, well thought of by all who knew him. He hadn't many friends, either. Except the members of my family and his brother. With those exceptions, we didn't mix much with people. We have known better times than these present ones, full of self-seeking and vulgarity...'

She straightened in her chair and gave him a look of proud dignity, as though she had known better days and better places.

'Your family...?'

'My father is still living. He is past seventy, in splendid health, and an ex-major in the army. I have also two sisters. My brother was killed in the First World War. A great loss...'

She was obviously on her favourite topic; reciting her pedigree and family glories. The kind of things she probably did when her husband was at home, running a failing business, depriving her of the life and ways to which she'd been accustomed before she married him.

'His brother...?'

'Is secretary of the local Water Board.'

She said it as though water was something undignified, and then she shut up, as though anxious to change the subject.

'How was... how was my husband...? How did he die?'

'He was stabbed, madam, and his body thrown in a flooded river. It was found soon afterwards by some passing farm-hands.'

'Farm-hands...?'

Another indignity!

'Were they the ones who killed and robbed him?'

'He was not robbed, madam. His things were all there, apparently untouched. We don't know yet who was responsible for the crime.'

Barbara was back.

'I've 'phoned them both. They'll be here in half an hour. Irene is seeing the headmaster right away. Chrissie says they have a man under gas and she won't be able to leave till he comes to...'

'Under gas...?'

Mrs. Teasdale didn't seem to understand.

'I also telephoned Grandfather. He's very upset. He says he wants to see the Superintendent right away. Could you manage that, Mr. Littlejohn? Grandfather is... well, he's the head of the family and now that father's gone... well...'

She burst into tears, too.

The two women, mother and daughter, embraced and wept on each other, and then Mrs. Teasdale broke away.

'We've to go to Lincoln…'

'Ely, madam.'

'It's the same… We've got to identify your father, Barbara… He's among strangers and we've to go and bring him home. The Superintendent and the local police are going to take us to him tonight. I really don't know how I can bear it. You must come and support me.'

'I'll have to let Alex know. I was meeting him tonight. Alex is my fiancé, Superintendent. He's a doctor. I'll have to telephone him. He'll be at the cottage hospital. All this has upset Alex very much…'

She hurried out again to telephone from the pub next door.

'A nice boy. They are very devoted. He's like a son to me…'

'Your two sisters are married?'

'Yes. One to a wholesale corn-merchant; the other to the local registrar of births, marriages, and deaths. Ought we to inform Walter?'

'Walter?'

'My brother-in-law. Walter Cornford. The registrar…'

'That will come later, madam. After the inquest.'

Barbara was back again. Still in her coat and dressing-gown. She looked a bit of a ragamuffin.

'Alex had just been operating on a man with hernia…'

'Barbara!'

'Well, it's his work. He's very upset. He says he doesn't approve of our going through such an ordeal. It's a man's job.'

Mrs. Teasdale took up a dramatic pose.

'No! He's my husband. I shall do it. You'd better ring up the family, Barbara. Uncle Walter, Uncle Sam… They'll be at their offices.

And tell Uncle Walter we'll report the death officially on our return. They'll tell Phoebe and Chloe.'

'What about Uncle Bertram?'

The man from the Water Board!

'Yes. Tell him, too. But ask him not to call round tonight. *Please*. I couldn't stand Bertram and Ethel just now. In fact, tell them *all* not to call. Tell them I'm going to Lincoln...'

'Ely.'

'It's the same. Tell them I'm going to Ely with the police to bring your father home. Tell them...'

Littlejohn was bewildered by the family ramifications. He lost track of the argument completely. He gathered that a meeting of the clans was threatened and that he might be involved in some awkward questions.

'I think perhaps I'd better call on the local police, Mrs. Teasdale, and report and also make arrangements for transport to Ely later this evening. Is there anything more I can do?'

The answer arrived in the shape of the landlord from the pub next door. A little fat man with a large waxed moustache, called Tinker. He entered the shop and stood there with the bell ringing until Barbara went to attend to him.

'Turn the lights on in the shop. It's getting dark...'

'We ought to close and put a ticket on the door, *Closed on Account of Death*, Mother.'

'Not *Death*, Barbara, *Bereavement*. It's more polite.'

And James Teasdale, alias Jim Lane, had found freedom from it all in running a show at the fair and living with a woman who looked like a gipsy! Littlejohn wondered what was going to happen when it all came out.

Barbara was dealing with the landlord in the shop. They could hear him whispering his message respectfully in the darkness beyond.

'Mr. Tinker says Grandfather's rung up. He wants to know why the Superintendent hasn't called. He says he wants to see him right away.'

'Does he live far away?'

'Five minutes on the 'bus. In the suburbs.'

'I'll get a police car to take me. What is the address?'

'The house is called *Rangoon*. It's on the Birkbeck Road.' Rangoon! That sounded ominous. Ex-Indian army?

'The police will know it?'

'Everybody knows Grandfather. Major Scott-Harris.'

'Very good. I'll go right away.'

Littlejohn thought of all the shocks and surprises Mrs. Teasdale was to suffer in the next few days. He'd better prepare her for some of them, whilst she was at home with her family to comfort her.

'You will have to be brave, Mrs. Teasdale, when the details of your husband's death are explained to you. Things are not quite what you would have expected.'

She stopped rocking and looked hard at him in the fading light.

Barbara switched on the light, which shone down from a shade made of beads and revealed the stark details of the room. The picture over the hearth with its sooty still-life, the bridal group, the untidy set-up with magazines, articles of clothing, even pairs of shoes and some corsets littered about on the floor and furniture.

'What do you mean?'

'He had evidently given up his post as representative of Oppenheimers, He had another job. Perhaps he hadn't told you?'

'No. Whatever was he doing? Surely nothing criminal.'

'Oh, no. He was running a hoop-la stall on fairgrounds.'

Mrs. Teasdale was on her feet, stabbing the air in Littlejohn's direction.

'What! What did I tell you? You've got the wrong man. It's absurd. Mistaken identity. James would never lower himself to such a thing. Fairground, indeed! Hoop-la! The police must be mad to think of it!'

'All the same, madam, it's true. You will find when you reach Ely and are able to see the body, that it is your husband.'

She didn't argue any more. It was evident that she preferred crime as her husband's new profession. Mrs. Teasdale just fainted away and gently sank back in the rocking-chair.

'Now look what you've done.'

Barbara began to flutter about. The shop bell rang again. A voice shouted 'All Right', presumably the family password, and Irene entered. She was more like her father than Barbara. Small-boned, fair, almost tiny in build, with the same strong glasses. She was vigorous in manner, too.

'Whatever's happening, here?'

'He's just told Mother that Father keeps a hoop-la stall on a fairground...'

Littlejohn excused himself and went off to see the old man from Rangoon.

4

FATHER

NOBODY ANSWERED LITTLEJOHN'S RING ON THE DOORBELL. Instead, a small sign on the doorpost lit up. Littlejohn could make out the words *Out, Engaged*, and *Enter*, in little frames on a contraption sometimes found on the office doors of business executives. It was *Enter* which was illuminated now. He turned the door-knob and found himself in the hall.

A large, old-fashioned house, with the smells of dust, kitchens, and dry rot fighting for supremacy. It stood in a vast garden surrounded by old untended trees, with a short gravel drive, and three stone steps leading to the front door. Squat in shape, it loomed out of the darkness from a background of tumbledown outhouses.

The Basilden police had provided a car for Littlejohn and it had pulled up at a gaslamp which shed a circle of light round the front gate of rusty wrought iron.

The local Superintendent had been very obliging and after discussing the formalities of the case had offered to accompany Littlejohn to see Major Scott-Harris, the dead man's father-in-law.

'Not that I relish the idea. He's a most unpleasant man. Always pestering us about trespassers and writing to the local paper about our inefficiency. We've never studied his army record, but I'd imagine he was a major in the Volunteers about the time of the Boer War...'

Littlejohn had decided to go alone. He liked it that way, especially as the old man hated the local police.

There was nobody in the hall, which was lighted by a small electric bulb in a charred parchment shade. It was large and barren-looking. At one side, a wide staircase. A bamboo hallstand; a chair like a bishop's which might have been rifled from a church; a long row of pegs on which were hung a strange variety of hats and coats, including a heavy cape; a threadbare Persian mat on the floor. Eastern weapons, daggers, spears, clubs hanging on the walls.

On the right, a glass-panelled door through the opaqueness of which Littlejohn could make out a red face and a bald head turned towards him. Nobody opened the door to meet him. Instead a man's voice, coarse, rusty, and loud called out:

'What do you want?'

Littlejohn opened the door and in a circle of light from a table lamp saw a man sitting in an armchair before the fire.

'Have you closed the front door?'

'Yes, sir.'

'Come in then and close that one, too.'

The man did not move. He was sprawling in the chair, his slippered feet on a footstool. At his elbow a glass and a bottle, and a syphon on the floor beside him. His filmy poached eyes looked his visitor over insolently, taking in every detail. Finally he pointed to a chair on the opposite side of the fire with a podgy hand.

'Sit down. You the police? I thought you'd come. It's taken you long enough.'

He spoke in short, brusque sentences, as though his breath were only sufficient for a few words at a time.

Was he seventy, or eighty? It was hard to guess. A monstrous fat man, with legs like the trunks of trees, and swollen hands. A square, livid face, with a bulbous nose lined with small red veins, and a short, thick neck.

The old man didn't move. He emptied his glass of whisky with a guzzling noise and passed his hand over the bottle and syphon.

'Help yourself and pour me another.'

He took a good drink when it was ready.

'I hear you're from Scotland Yard. Local chaps are quite incompetent. Good thing you're here.'

'As the crime was committed in the east of England and as the place is flooded, I'm giving them a hand.'

'So, it's true, then. Jim's got himself murdered. I told Elvira when she married him, he'd come to a bad end. No good for anything. How did it happen? I telephoned the local police, but they said they'd no details. It's like 'em to know nothing about it.'

Littlejohn told him how James Teasdale had met his death.

'That's all, so far, sir.'

'No clues?'

'No, sir.'

'I suppose you've called to ask me some questions. Fire away.'

Scott-Harris turned his congested face the better to see Littlejohn. His large sensual mouth opened every time he drew in a breath, as though his nose were inadequate to cater for his huge frame.

'Was Teasdale a native of these parts?'

'Yes. His father was a cashier in a mill. Fancied themselves off nothing. Jim never had a proper job. First it was an arts and crafts shop. What a set-up! Then photography... No good at either. Then, he started as a commercial traveller. Seemed to do a bit better at that. I wouldn't be surprised if there wasn't some jiggery-pokery about that job. It surprised me that he made money in it. It needs personality to be a good salesman, which was precisely what Jim hadn't got.'

He changed his position in the chair, panting and grunting as he did so. Major Scott-Harris was a sensualist to his finger tips. He believed in an easy life. He'd married a wife with money of her own, unfortunately for him, locked up in a trust. But she'd left her income and three daughters to him. The girls had cosseted him until they married. He hardly raised a hand to help himself.

'What was Jim doing when he was killed? Not commercial travelling, I'll bet.'

'He ran a profitable sideshow at fairs.'

Old Scott-Harris couldn't believe it. He clawed the air and seemed to hoist himself upright by it. Then he laughed. A hoarse, bubbling noise from deep in his chest.

'I'll be damned! I thought as much. Didn't I say jiggery-pokery? And I'll bet he kept another establishment, too. Didn't he?'

'He had a woman assisting him.'

'I'll bet he did! I told Elvira. But she wouldn't believe me. I didn't know he had it in him.'

'I take it you objected to their marriage, sir.'

'Like hell, I did. Elvira met him at an arts and crafts class. You'd have thought the feller was an R.A. Big bowtie, arty clothes, full of swank. And depending on his parents for a living. Elvira was the prim, plain Jane of the family. Hadn't had a man about her before. The little pipsqueak seemed to rush her off her feet. When they said they were engaged, I refused to agree. He hadn't even got a job. Only a scholarship to take him to some London art school. He said he'd give up the idea of taking up the scholarship and settle down in an arts and crafts shop. I showed him the door.'

'But you eventually agreed.'

'I never agreed...'

His colour rose. Littlejohn thought he was going to have a fit. The major took a good gulp of whisky to restore him.

'... He put Elvira in the family way. They had to get married...'

So, it had been a shotgun wedding, after all!

'A big splash of a weddin', too. His family must have spent all their savings on it. They didn't get a penny from me. I gave 'em a copper kettle for a weddin' present and told 'em they'd made their bed and could lie in it.'

'But, according to your daughter, they became reconciled to you.'

'They visited me here, if that's what you mean. But I couldn't bear the sight of the feller.'

'I see.'

'You see, do you? Well, that's nothing to do with Jim getting himself killed, has it? What exactly do you want to know?'

'You asked to see *me*, sir. What do *you* want to know?'

'Pour me another glass. Take one yourself, too. You seem a decent sort. Here's good health to you, anyway. I hope you solve the case. Don't like mysteries. I want to know who killed Jim, that's all. Asked you to come here to tell you what I thought about Jim and that I won't have a lot of dirty linen washed in public. Our family stands high around here. Don't want any scandals.'

Littlejohn was sure it stood high. Or, at least Scott-Harris thought it did. Bullying and browbeating everyone, as though he were feudal lord of the place. And James Teasdale hadn't been good enough for a Scott-Harris daughter. No doubt the major had told him so many times. Especially when things were bad for him financially. So, James has sought other ways of success – on fairgrounds.

'Had Teasdale any enemies locally?'

'Enemies? No. Not the type. To have enemies you need to promote hatred. You need to have some personality which makes 'em object to you. Jim had no personality. People didn't hate him. They just brushed him aside.'

'Indeed! From what I gather elsewhere, he seemed a decent kind of fellow. He was well thought of in the places he visited.'

'Decent, did you say? Decent? And him running a show on a fairground and living with another woman. Do you call that decent? Had he any other children on the wrong side of the blanket?'

'No. We don't even know that the woman was his mistress. Her name was Martha Gomm and she seems a very kindly, hard-working sort.'

'Martha Gomm! Good God! What a name.'

It certainly wasn't hyphenated and it was short enough. Littlejohn was beginning to understand why James Teasdale had fled to the fairgrounds of the south. His father-in-law was enough to make any man take to his heels, to say nothing of his own family.

'You'd no idea what he was doing to keep his family in decent circumstances then, Major Scott-Harris?'

'I had not. But I guessed there was something queer about it. Told Elvira as much. Runnin' off every week on what he called his rounds. Then, back at week-end, and off again. It wasn't normal. Why did he keep the shop goin'? Why didn't he take his family nearer his work, instead of scuttering here and there like a rabbit? Now, I know why. Well, I'm not surprised.'

He tossed his fat hand about in the air and coughed asthmatically as though the effort were too much for him.

'It didn't worry me, though. As I said, I told 'em they'd made their bed. I take things as they come. Man of the world. Can't say I'm surprised. Elvira isn't what you'd call a feminine woman. No charm. I'd say she ran after Teasdale and more or less forced him into marriage. She's my own daughter and I suppose it's wrong to say it, but she's not cut out for keeping a man... The rest are the same. Two other daughters, Phoebe and Chloe...'

He cleared his throat. The whisky was making him talk a lot. In fact, he was getting sorry for himself – pitying himself for having three daughters without charm.

'... Phoebe's married to a corn merchant. He poses as a miller, but he's not. Sells corn by the stone to hen-keepers and seeds by the packet for owners of budgerigars. Chloe, the youngest, married the local registrar of births, marriages and deaths. What a trio of sons-in-law! It's enough to make a man damn well shoot himself.'

'You were in the regular army, sir?'

Littlejohn said it for lack of anything else to talk about.

'No. Territorial. Joined up in the first war. Retired when I returned in '19. Now I'm all on me own.'

He passed his glass over to Littlejohn and inclined his head in the direction of the bottle. If there was anyone else around, he presumably did nothing for himself.

'My family's a very old one. Sometimes feel ashamed how the present generations have lowered the standards. It's because there are so many damn' women in the family now. I'd a son, but he was killed in Burma in the last war...'

He paused and breathed hard.

'The rest were girls. Three girls. And they've not produced a son among them. What the hell's the matter with the family? Nobody but girls. Elvira has three and Phoebe and Chloe, one girl apiece. I was surprised about Elvira, I must say. After the third girl in four years, I gave the pair of 'em a talkin'-to. Stop it! I told 'em. That's quite enough. Looks as if they did as I advised 'em...'

'They'll be a comfort to Mrs. Teasdale now, I suppose.'

'Comfort! Hah! That's what's caused the family to deteriorate. Women who'd take anybody for a husband. Elvira, a penniless painter. Phoebe, a corn seller. Chloe, a registrar of births and such like. And now, Elvira's girl, Irene's knocking about with a bookie. Can you wonder the family standard's declined?'

To hear him talk, you'd have thought he came from a family of ancient dukes. Instead, here he was, an old soak, full of his own importance, trying to give the impression he'd seen better days.

'You live alone, sir?'

'Got a batman, who lives in. He takes every evenin' out. Can't keep servants these days unless you pander to 'em. That's why I put the indicator thing on the front door. Saw 'em advertised somewhere. It's a damn' good idea. Saves me having to answer the door myself.'

'Was this man your batman in the war?'

'No. He's been in the army though, and we understand one another. The girls call to see me regularly, although none of them will do a hand's turn in the house. I have a daily woman to help Ryder. He should be in any time…'

A pause. There was hardly a sound from the street outside. They might have been right in the country instead of almost in the town itself. In one corner, a grandfather clock ticked away the time. It was almost seven o'clock. Littlejohn realised he hadn't eaten since his meal in the train between Ely and Sheffield.

'I'm glad you've called, Superintendent. We've had a heart to heart talk and you know how I'm placed myself and what I think of my family. All the girls are plain Janes, who've taken a motley lot of husbands for the sake of being married…'

No wonder! If this was the best the Major could do, it wasn't surprising his daughters had taken the first chance of going to the altar!

'As for Jim… He didn't like being called Jim. He was always known as James at home. I liked calling him Jim just to rile him. Well, as for Jim, I can't believe it's happened. To get murdered after years of earning money on a fairground and living tally with another woman. It beats me.'

'He was perhaps driven to it. After all, with a bankrupt business and a growing family, he must have been desperate.'

Scott-Harris moved brusquely for the first time, just to enable him to slap his hand down hard on the table.

'Desperate! He's let down the family, sir. Made a laughing stock of me. He deserved all he got.'

And with that he slumped down in his chair again.

'Are you confined indoors all the time, sir?'

'No. I go out in the car now and then in the daytime. But I'm whacked at night. Had enough. Spend the evenin's indoors.'

What a life! The coal fire was half-way up the chimney, scorching everything within two yards of the fireplace. The room smelled stuffy and airless. The reek of whisky hung heavily about the place. And Major Scott-Harris... Theobald Scott-Harris according to the inscription on a plate screwed to a clock on the mantelpiece... It wasn't going and had been presented to him by his fellow J.P.s on the Basilden bench in 1948.

Scott-Harris began to struggle in his chair and before Littlejohn quite realised what he was doing, he was on his feet. He looked far worse upright than reclining. Huge, monstrously corpulent, sagging with his own weight. He wobbled to the sideboard, unlocked a drawer with a key from his pocket, and produced a box of cigars.

'Have one. Got to lock 'em up. Ryder's too fond of cigars...'

He cut and lit one himself and Littlejohn did the same. He didn't feel like it on an empty stomach, but it was something to do.

'As I said, I'm glad you came. It's been a bit of company for me. Couldn't have stood the local police. If I'd still been on the bench, I'd have smartened them up. As it is, they'd have called with a lot of silly questions, written 'em down in a book, asked me to sign it, and then gone off without a word of thanks.'

'They're busy these days, sir. So much petty crime and violence about and too few constables to attend to it. They do their best.'

'Might have known you'd take their side. However, I still have my own ideas...'

Scott-Harris puffed his cigar and his head slowly nodded. Before Littlejohn realised what had happened, the old man was asleep.

The cigar fell from his fingers and Littlejohn picked it up from the threadbare carpet and put it safely in an ash-tray. The Major was snoring quietly, his mouth open.

Littlejohn looked around him. A pretty kettle of fish! All alone in the house with the owner asleep, alternating his snores with the ticking of the clock in the corner.

Out-of-date furniture in heavy Victorian style. More trophies from the Far East on the walls. A cavalry sabre, crossed swords, and some daggers. Funny stuff for a non-regular soldier to collect. But perhaps Scott-Harris liked to give the impression that he'd travelled far. On the mantelpiece in a wooden frame a photograph of a young man with a long, eager face and a pleasant smile, dressed as a Second Lieutenant of the last war. On the other, a portrait of a sad-eyed woman, who must have been Mrs. Scott-Harris. It was fading in a nimbus of photographic chemicals. Perhaps the work of her late son-in-law, Teasdale.

The Superintendent wondered what to do. If he left the old man asleep, he might easily turn and fall in the fire. Or perhaps this was what happened every evening after Ryder had gone for his night out. Scott-Harris made himself half-drunk and then fell asleep until the man wakened him on his return.

The problem was solved by the noise of footsteps approaching the front door. A key was inserted in the lock and the door creaked open.

Littlejohn met the newcomer on the mat. A little thin man in a coat a size too large for him and a black slouch hat. The light of the hall lit up his bright dark eyes and his cheeky expression. About fifty or thereabouts, with a thin hatchet face, a mean mouth, and a large nose, once broken and badly set. Probably the man who filched Scott-Harris's cigars and, when he'd the chance, his whisky as well.

'Hullo… Been callin'?'

'Good evening. I've just been to see Major Scott-Harris. My name's Littlejohn. Superintendent Littlejohn, of Scotland Yard.'

The man whistled.

'So they've got the Yard in already. I heard about Jimmie Teasdale's murder. Bit of a surprise, isn't it?'

'Major Scott-Harris is asleep, so I thought I'd better leave him in peace.'

'Been giving him a grilling?'

'That's no business of yours, Ryder.'

'Sorry. He often falls off and I find him sleepin' off his whisky by the fire when I get in. Lucky I got back early tonight. I've just been an errand. Finished your business with him?'

'Yes.'

'Did he treat you civil?'

'What do you mean?'

'He's a tartar if he takes a dislike to anybody.'

'Does he get out much, or is he mainly confined indoors?'

'He goes out in the car now and then. Wonderfully active, considerin' his age and his bulk. Always stays in of an evenin'. Likes it by the fire with his glass. By the time it gets six o'clock, he's after the whisky, though I must say, he rarely touches it in the day, except with his lunch. A man of routine, is the major.'

'I'm just on my way.'

'The police car's waitin' for you, there. It must be something important if they've got you chaps from the Yard on it. Why anybody should want to murder Jimmie Teasdale, I can't think. Always liked him although the gov'nor didn't. Couldn't stand the sight of him. Only last week-end, he showed him the door, after they'd had a row. I don't know what it was about, but the gov'nor took on badly with him. The major always said Jimmie was a no-good. I didn't

agree with him. I always thought Jimmie did his best. A chap can't
do more, can he?'

The voice had a whining note and Ryder had an unpleasant habit
of thrusting his face close to Littlejohn's as he spoke. His breath
was heavy with beer.

Littlejohn had had enough. He opened the door and let himself
out, made for the waiting car, and left Ryder standing on the mat.

It was raining now and the gas-lamps threw long shafts of light
across the wet roads and pavements. In a public hall a few doors away
they were dancing and the blare of saxophones came through the
open door. In Scott-Harris's garden some cats were fighting and, in
their citadel, somewhere in the darkness, the Salvation Army band
were playing *Onward, Christian Soldiers*.

5

FAMILY COUNCIL

T HE POLICE CAR DREW UP AT THE SHOP IN HIGH STREET. A vehicle and driver had been ordered for Littlejohn at the police station and he had arranged to take Mrs. Teasdale and her eldest daughter with him to Ely to identify the body.

Bertram, James's brother, had been waiting for the Superintendent at the police station, as well. He seemed annoyed at Littlejohn for being so long away. He wasn't a bit like the dead man. Tall, beefy, bull-necked, florid. He'd been described as secretary of the local Water Board, but he didn't seem a good advertisement for their products. His nose was large and glowing. Maybe, he took water with his whisky, but it was unlikely, judging from the results. He was bald and very conscious of it. He was rarely seen without his hat. Some people even suggested that he slept in it.

'Can we 'ush this up?' Bertram asked Littlejohn almost at once.

Littlejohn raised his eyebrows. It was as much as he could do not to laugh outright.

'Don't get me wrong. I want justice done. Who wouldn't when his own brother's been murdered? But all this 'oop-la business. Is it necessary to bring that in? It would embarrass the family no end.'

'I think it showed your brother in a good light, Mr. Teasdale, if I may say so. He wasn't making enough to bring up his family as he liked in his business, so he put his pride in his pocket and went off and took a job on a fairground. He'd got guts, I must say.'

Bertram looked uneasy.

'I admit that. He was only the size of six pennyworth of copper, but, as you say, he'd always got guts. He'd take on chaps twice his size when he was a kid. I grant you that. But I'm told by the police here, that there was some other woman involved. I can't believe it. He wasn't that sort at all. There must have been some mistake.'

'It's quite true. She helped him at the fair and took charge of his pitch for him when he came north to see his family.'

'Were they carryin' on together?'

Bertram's nose glowed. Perhaps he was admiring his brother's audacity, but he daren't say so.

'I couldn't say, sir. I didn't ask. She seemed a decent sort of woman and thought the world of your brother.'

Bertram's bleary eyes projected from their sockets with emotion.

'He'd gone potty, I do declare. To run off and behave the way he did. But I always said what it would be. A snobby wife and three girls always nagging at him and looking down on him, and old Scott-Harris bullying him about not making a success of his life. It drove him round the bend.'

'Wasn't he happily married?'

Bertram shrugged his heavy shoulders.

'He never said as much. He was always loyal to Elvira. But the tastes she had and the extravagant way she brought up the girls... It was scandalous. He borrowed money from me now and then. He paid it off later, after he got... well... he said he was travelling for a Manchester business house. He *was* travellin', too! To some tune, he was. 'Oop-la and livin' with another woman. I never heard anythin' like it!'

He looked puzzled and melancholy now. As though he'd got the sack from the waterworks!

'You don't like the Scott-Harris family?'

'I do not. He never ought to have got mixed-up with them. They're a conceited lot, off nothing. Who *is* Scott-Harris? A major in the Territorials, that's all. Lived on his wife's money. Before he married her he was a penniless auctioneer, who never did another stroke of work after he wed Beatrice Dutton...'

'Did James get on well with his wife's family?'

'They always looked down on him. Her father actually called him a no-good bum. *He'd* a lot to talk about. Elvira set her cap at James from the start. He was her only chance, if you ask me. There was a baby on the way and they had to get married.'

Mr. Bertram Teasdale passed his hand across his lips. He felt like a drink.

'Care to finish this talk over a drink at the club?'

'I'm sorry, sir. I've got to pick up Mrs. Teasdale and take her to Ely to identify her husband's body.'

'So I hear. I rang her up and offered to do it myself. After all, I'm his only brother. But, no. She was determined to go herself. It was her duty, she said. Now that James is dead, she's suddenly begun to talk about her duty. She'd no such ideas when he was alive.'

It ended there and Littlejohn went off to the shop.

The door was locked but there were lights showing in the inner room. Littlejohn noticed a bell-push on the doorjamb and pressed it. He saw the door to the back room open, and cast a shaft of light in the dark confusion of the deserted shop. It dimly illuminated a framed picture which looked to have been extracted from a Christmas almanac.

It was ten o'clock and still raining. The dismal streets were quiet and the main road which passed the shop looked like a sheet of glass under the poor electric lights which hung from old disused tramway-standards overhead. A few cars passed. In the pub next door, someone was playing a tinny piano and they were singing a sentimental chorus. *There's an old mill by the stream, Nellie Dean...*

The shop door opened after someone had turned the key and rattled a chain. The girl who answered must have been Christine, Teasdale's youngest. Another bouncing wench, who took after her mother. Fair, lazy-looking, plump, easy-going.

'Come in, sir.'

More polished than the rest. Probably through associating with the best dentist in the town and his patients.

The shop was in darkness and smelled of arts and crafts.

In the room behind there was a babel of voices. It sounded as if, in spite of Mrs. Teasdale's wishes, her family had descended upon her. All the girls were at home and, in addition, two women and their husbands. It was obvious that the women were Elvira's sisters. All three of them looked alike, except that differences in age and circumstances had given them different lines of character. In fact, all six women, in some queer way, bore traces of Major Scott-Harris. No wonder James Teasdale had run away and fetched up on a fairground with Martha Gomm! It must have been more than flesh and blood could bear!

Mrs. Teasdale ceremonially introduced Littlejohn all round. For some reason, he felt they regarded him as on their side and they treated him cordially.

'I can't understand it at all. A hoop-la stall!'

That was Phoebe, the second sister, whose husband was reputed to be better off than the rest and who always said the first things which came to her mind. The comment was supposed to indicate to Littlejohn that James was an outsider and had disgraced the family. Chloe, the youngest of the Scott-Harris daughters, was normally fat and jolly. Now she was wearing a long face and endorsing all that Phoebe said.

The corn-chandler was a heavy man who wore a deep white collar and a heavy watchchain across his paunch. Another bald head, with hairy ears.

'I've always expected something of this sort from Jim. He wasn't stable. These arty chaps are all alike.'

Mrs. Teasdale began to sob again and mopped her eyes and red nose with a damp handkerchief.

'He's disgraced us all.'

Not a word of sympathy for the murdered man. He might have engineered it all specially to spite them.

The registrar of births, marriages and deaths was sitting in the rocking-chair, heaving himself to and fro miserably.

'This has put paid to the old-tyme dancing contest,' he suddenly said.

The rest turned on him. He was small and dapper, with well-greased dark hair, probably discreetly dyed, and a small grey moustache. He looked like a shopwalker.

'Walter!'

His wife thought she ought to explain to Littlejohn.

'We indulge in dancing to keep our weight down. We are this year's champion pair in Basilden and are competing at the all-England festival. Now, of course... Well, it wouldn't be right, would it?'

The corn-chandler bit the end off a cigar, spat it in the fire, and struck a match, which he held burning in his fingers.

'I'm surprised at you two, at your ages. Dancing! It's not decent.'

He puffed angrily at his cigar.

The doorbell rang again and Irene answered it. Her face glowed as she went, for she thought it was the bookie who was courting her calling to express his condolences. Instead it was the potman from next door.

'Major Scott-Harris has telephoned to ask if Mrs. Teasdale's left to identify the body, yet?'

The corn-chandler looked alarmed.

'Tell him, yes… We don't want him down here, tonight. If he calls, it'll only end up in another family row. Tell him she's gone.'

The potman cast a look of surprise and reproach on the chandler and left. Mr. Sam Geddes was a deacon of his chapel. The potman was disappointed in him!

It gave Littlejohn a chance to remind Mrs. Teasdale that they'd a long night's journey to make.

'I've been telling Elvira, that I ought to go with her, not Barbara…'

Phoebe again! That must have been the cause of the family row which had hushed when Littlejohn entered. In reply, Barbara went from the room and returned with her hat and coat on. She was lugging a large shabby suitcase, too. From the looks of it, the pair of them intended staying at Ely for a week or two. Mrs. Teasdale regarded the suitcase with horrified eyes. It bore the initials J.T. They had used it on their honeymoon!

'Not that one!'

'Why not? What's wrong with it? The other's full of winter underwear.'

Littlejohn carried it to the car for them.

'Have you had a meal, Superintendent? I'm afraid we've only some cold Cornish pasties to offer, but…'

He hastily said he'd eaten. The Basilden police had given him tea and some large ham sandwiches. In any case, he'd have declined. All the way to Ely on cold pasties was more than his digestion could endure!

The departing pair were seen off by the whole family. There was kissing all round. An orgy of it. Chloe, the frisky olde-tyme dancer, looked ready to kiss Littlejohn. If she started, he'd have to go through the lot. He hurried to the car. They packed the women and their belongings and then there were more farewells. It was turning-out time at the pub next door and the send-off party was joined by a number of half-tipsy men and women, some of whom wept when they knew what was going on.

The pious corn-chandler pronounced the benediction.

'Bear up, Elvira. It'll soon be over. God bless you. We'll look after everything...'

It was a nightmare journey. There were several diversions on the way in places where the roads were under water. The rain had ceased but they passed flooded fields and swollen rivers all along the route. The pair on the back seat seemed to sleep fitfully. Now and then, one of them would come to life.

'Where are we? How long yet?'

They stopped about half a dozen times, when Mrs. Teasdale got out, saying she had cramp.

'I've always been troubled with it. Sometimes, I've thought I'd die with it. For nights on end, James had to get up with me and walk me up and down; it was so bad.'

Night and day, poor Teasdale seemed to have had no peace!

They reached Ely at breakfast time. Cromwell was waiting for Littlejohn at the police station. It was like a tonic to see him after the horror of the journey. Littlejohn lit the pipe he hadn't been able to smoke on the way. Mrs. Teasdale, it seemed, had a sensitive throat. She'd told him so as soon as she'd seen him filling his pipe. She looked years older and was dishevelled from the journey. On the other hand, the dark misty patches under Barbara's eyes gave her a mysterious added oriental charm, as though she'd been using mascara.

'Where have they put him?'

Barbara was impatient with her mother and snapped her up.

'What about some breakfast first?'

Both women ate a good meal of bacon and eggs, after which Mrs. Teasdale was ready for business.

'I don't understand why anybody wanted to kill James.'

'We'll try to find out, Mrs. Teasdale.'

'I still think it's a matter of mistaken identity. When I see the body, I'm sure it won't be his.'

Outside, the sun was struggling through a mist which rose from the sodden earth. The cathedral towered over the housetops. People were about their business on the streets as though everything were ordinary and the tragedies of the floods and murder were far away. Now and then a squad of police or firemen rushed past in a car.

A police sergeant called to take them to the mortuary.

'I can't face it.'

Mrs. Teasdale stood like someone in a trance at the door of the hotel.

Barbara took her in hand.

'What have we come all this way for? Pull yourself together.'

Opposite the mortuary was a café in which people were drinking morning coffee and reading the daily papers. Mrs. Teasdale seemed to see nothing of what was going on around her. She was concentrating on the task in hand, her lips in a firm line, her leather handbag tightly gripped in her fingers.

The coroner's officer joined them and muttered condolences. Mrs. Teasdale didn't seem to hear. Barbara thanked him instead.

Littlejohn dreaded his second meeting with the dead man. Now, that he knew more about him, he was filled with compassion for him. James Teasdale had been knocked about from pillar to post by his wife and her family; dogged by ill-luck in business. A no-good bum, his father-in-law had called him. Then, he'd found a bit of peace with Martha Gomm and some respite from his creditors and his extravagant family in a job which the Scott-Harris clan couldn't believe existed. He'd fled from the torture of the life in Basilden and found happiness in a roving existence. And now he'd ended up on the slab in the morgue…

They were there. The attendant and the rest were speaking in whispers. The body was on a trolley covered by a sheet. Mrs. Teasdale stood for a second, holding her breath. Then she looked at the calm face of the dead man.

She didn't even cry out. Neither did Barbara, who peeped over her shoulder. They were all waiting for what the widow was going to do. Her reaction was surprising. She turned brusquely to Littlejohn.

'It is my husband. How dare they strip him naked? I never saw him naked before in my life. He was not that sort…'

Barbara wondered what was coming next. She hastily took her mother by the arm and led her out. The men in attendance gave each other blank looks. One of them shrugged his shoulders and smiled.

'She's a queer one. Not a tear or a sigh. Instead, she's worrying about him bein' in his birthday suit!'

Littlejohn stooped and picked up the black leather handbag which had slipped from Mrs. Teasdale's hands as she faced her dead husband. The leather still bore the marks – eight of them – where she had driven her fingernails as she faced the ordeal.

'At a time like this, people don't know what they're saying. They say anything,' he said. And he followed the widow into the open air.

6

TICKET TO NORWICH

LITTLEJOHN WAS QUITE AT A LOSS. THE CORONER HAD adjourned the inquest after Mrs. Teasdale had given evidence of identification and the police surgeon had made his report. The doctor seemed sure of only one thing; that Teasdale had been murdered. And, of course, that probably an hour or two before he died, he'd eaten a meal of corned beef and tomatoes, and washed it down with tea. The time of death was uncertain. The body had been immersed and tossed about in the cold waters of the river. Temperature was, therefore, not a sure way of determining the precise hour.

Cromwell had carefully checked the movements of everybody who might have been concerned and had business with Teasdale. It might have been reasonable to think that Martha Gomm and Teasdale had quarrelled and that she had stabbed him. But Martha Gomm could account for her movements between six in the morning and the time she'd met Littlejohn. She said she had been awakened at an early hour by the floods and that she and her landlady had been together, engaged in salvage and precautions all the rest of the day. Mrs. Southery and a number of villagers with whom she had worked confirmed it.

Corned beef and tomatoes! And according to medical evidence, eaten an hour or two before death. Cromwell, with his usual energetic initiative had, during Littlejohn's absence, enquired in most of the cafés in Ely if Teasdale had eaten there on the day he died. An hour might have passed quite reasonably between his eating in Ely and reaching the spot where he'd been murdered. No results.

The rescued rattletrap of a car found by the riverside, the car in which Teasdale and Martha Gomm had travelled from fair to fair, had been carefully examined. The only reason for its giving out had, according to experts, been shortage of petrol. The tank was empty.

Mrs. Teasdale had recovered her equanimity very quickly after her visit to the mortuary. She had appeared in the coroner's court spruce and tidy and had given her evidence sensibly and clearly. No scenes; no tears. She attached herself to Littlejohn as they left the court.

'What do we do now? Can I take his poor body home with me?'

'Yes. I gather the undertakers have made all arrangements. It is already in a coffin and can travel on the same train with you, if you wish.'

'I would like that.'

The formalities were ended and there was a train at two o'clock or thereabouts. They had booked a room for Mrs. Teasdale at The Bell, although she wasn't staying the night. She and Barbara seemed without friends and forlorn and Littlejohn suggested that they lunched with him and Cromwell at the hotel.

'I think Mother would like to lie down in her room till train time. Perhaps they would send up a light meal and some tea for her. I'm sure she doesn't feel like eating much...'

They arranged it the way Barbara suggested and the remaining three of them took their meal in the dining-room.

Littlejohn didn't know what to do next. Did the solution lie at Martha Gomm's end of Teasdale's affairs; or was it hidden somewhere back at Basilden?

Over coffee, he opened the matter again.

'Do you feel able to answer a few more questions, Miss Barbara?'

Barbara and her mother, for that matter, didn't seem prostrated by Teasdale's death. They took it very philosophically. Perhaps because he'd been so little at home in late years and they'd managed to do without him. His many absences had almost divorced him from the family in High Street and now that the first shock was over, they had quickly recovered.

Barbara even smiled.

'Yes. I want to help to clear matters up. Whoever committed the crime oughtn't to get away with it.'

'What time, then, did your father leave home on Sunday evening?'

'Around seven o'clock. Irene hadn't long been gone to church, which starts at 6.30.'

'Did he usually come home in his car?'

'Yes. It was a bit of a disgrace and we tried to persuade him to buy another, even if he'd to get it on the H.P. But he said the one he had was all right and gave him very little trouble. It was an old one, I know.'

Probably Teasdale had thought a new car too opulent for his use at fairs and had stuck to the old one. Of course, his family hadn't known that and he hadn't been able to explain. Littlejohn could well imagine the family, particularly Barbara and her medical consultant, wishing he'd change it and stop putting them to shame!

'He left in it last Sunday?'

'Yes. He garaged it in a wooden shed in the yard behind the shop.'

'Did he have a meal before he left home?'

'Yes. The doctor mentioned it in court.'

Littlejohn paused in filling his pipe.

'Corned beef and tomatoes. I felt so ashamed. It sounded so common. But he'd had a good high tea at about five. Then, about half an hour before he was due to go, Mother told me he said he'd better have a snack, as it would be breakfast before he ate again. We'd only tinned stuff in. The joint was finished for lunch. He liked corned beef and had a weakness for tomatoes.'

She talked on and on, excusing herself for the vulgarity of the contents of the dead man's stomach, which had come out so pointedly in the coroner's court.

Littlejohn wasn't listening.

Teasdale's supper had only been half digested when he died. And his body had been found in the Dumb River. He could not have covered the distance from Basilden in an hour.

So, someone had brought his dead body there!

Cromwell had understood, too.

'Had I better tell the local police to let the Tylecote people know you're going back to Basilden, sir?'

'Please do, old man. And then go back to Tylecote and see if you can find anything more about Mr. Teasdale's movements and background there and on his travels. Talk with Martha Gomm again...'

Barbara paused with her coffee cup half-way to her lips.

'Martha Gomm? Whoever's that?'

'The woman who worked for him at the fairgrounds. She looked after the stall when he was away. You saw her in court this morning.'

Barbara blushed and looked him in the eyes angrily. She understood, but didn't say any more.

'I'll go and see to Mother.'

'Very good. We'll meet in the porch. I'll order a taxi to the station.'

He was sorry when the time came and he had to say good-bye to Cromwell.

'Telephone me at the Basilden police station, old chap. If you exhaust the possibilities in Tylecote, I'll probably ask you to join me in the north. I'll need some moral support, I'm sure.'

It was dark when they reached Basilden. A coffin-car was waiting for the remains of James Teasdale. Here, he wasn't Jim Lane, fairground operative, any more. He was James Teasdale, commercial traveller, Jack-of-all-trades, the no-good bum, as old Scott-Harris called him...

The coffin was going to someone's funeral parlour for the night, until arrangements could be made.

The journey north had seemed interminable. Littlejohn had spent much of the time in the corridor smoking his pipe, the very sight of which had made Mrs. Teasdale start coughing. She had sat silent for most of the way, gripping her black leather handbag, now and then shedding a few tears. Sometimes, she'd speak, mainly about funeral arrangements. Who to invite, where to hold it, the pros and cons of cremation or burial. She'd even got the menu for the meal afterwards. By the time they reached Sheffield, it had all been tidily arranged. Barbara had made a list of mourners and memoranda about the sequence of events. A schedule of the day's formalities.

The station was deserted and the funeral men performed their duties in silence, reverently panting and heaving as they unloaded the remains. The stationmaster was on duty and arrived to express his condolences with the widow. He was a tall, dyspeptic-looking man with a long red nose and sighed again and again as he watched the gruesome task unfolding. Now and then, he warned the handlers to be careful. The engine driver was impatient to be off. He was late already. He even left his locomotive to find the guard and complain. 'We've not got all night. I could have done it quicker myself.'

Littlejohn took the stationmaster aside.

'I'd like a word with you later, in private.'

The stationmaster examined him carefully under the gas-lamp.

'I'll have to see this business over first.'

He was sucking peppermint lozenges and breathed a blast over Littlejohn.

'Later, then. When the ladies have gone.'

Littlejohn saw them off in a taxi.

'I'll follow on foot.'

The stationmaster was called McHarry and led Littlejohn to his office. A small, stuffy room, smelling of peppermint and old air, littered with forms and ornamented with ancient posters. *Come to Skegness. Blackpool in the Autumn. Five Days in Paris for Ten Pounds.* That must have been a long time ago!

'Well, sir. I suppose you represent the police.'

'My name's Littlejohn. Superintendent Littlejohn, of Scotland Yard.'

It put the stationmaster out of countenance. He whistled.

'By jove! They intend to find out who did for poor Teasdale, don't they? Scotland Yard, eh? That'll give them something to talk about!'

And he rooted about until he'd found a moth-eaten old cushion and placed it on his official plain-wood chair.

'Sit down, sir.'

'I just wanted to ask you if you'd issued any tickets to one place or another lately.'

'We issue them to all over the country here. You'd be surprised.'

Littlejohn took out an old envelope on which he'd copied out the recent schedule of Teasdale's fairground visits.

Lowestoft, Banbury, Blisworth, Evesham, Midhurst...

Mr. McHarry looked flabbergasted.

'What's all this about?'

'It's confidential, but I assure you, has to do with the case we're on about the murder of James Teasdale.'

The stationmaster looked at Littlejohn as if he'd gone mad. He took off his official cap and slapped his bald head as though trying to stimulate his brain to a clearer understanding. He looked better without his cap, which was a size too large for him.

'Well, you know best, but it seems queer to me.'

He took out a bunch of keys and went and opened an old safe under a desk along one side of the dismal room. Then he turned and brought with him a large dog-eared book. His stomach rumbled in protest and he slipped another white tablet in his mouth.

'This is the record of tickets issued. Blessed if we've issued tickets to any of those places in the last few weeks. They're summer resorts by the sound of them. Nobody in Basilden wants to go so far at this time of year. However, we can only have a look.'

He cleared a space among the decaying waybills and circulars which loaded the desk and began to thumb the ledger.

It took a long time. Mr. McHarry was a resolute and finicky man. When he made a statement, he was always sure it was right. He checked the entries three times before he made a pronouncement.

'We've not issued any tickets to those places since summer. Before then, I wouldn't know without going back in the book.'

There was a large map of the British Isles on the wall, flyblown and soiled from many years of hanging there. Littlejohn went over to it and stood contemplating it. Mr. McHarry joined him and contemplated it with him. They sought and found each of the places on Littlejohn's list. It seemed a forlorn search. Littlejohn was wondering if anyone who knew Teasdale in Basilden had visited one of the fairs and come upon James Lane at his hoop-la pitch and had somehow become involved in the great deception.

He drew an imaginary circle round each place and examined the towns within it. Mr. McHarry stood breathing down his collar, wondering what eccentricity his visitor was up to.

Then they began to play a kind of game. Littlejohn recited the names of towns near Teasdale's stopping-places at fairs and Mr. McHarry looked in his book.

'No... None there... Nothing to Oxford. Nothing to Leamington...'

The stationmaster was getting rattled. Trains came and went and the porter on the platform kept entering and leaving the office with queries and questions, which his inquisitive mind had concocted to enable him to find out what was going on. He received no satisfaction. In the end, Mr. McHarry, exasperated by events, told him to clear off and stay out. The porter withdrew, contemplating making a complaint to his union.

'Norwich…' It wasn't far from Lowestoft.

Mr. McHarry almost shouted with triumph.

'Yes! Second return, exactly ten days ago.'

'Can you tell me who you issued it to?'

The stationmaster sighed wearily.

'I'm not the booking-clerk. He's gone off duty and I'm only doing it temporary tonight because his wife's having a baby and I let him off, see? But I think I know who booked it. It was Harry Wood.'

'Who's Harry Wood?'

The stationmaster obviously pitied Littlejohn for his ignorance.

'He's the best bass singer for miles round here. He's won prizes at musical festivals all over the country. It was in the local paper that he was going singing at Norwich musical festival. He didn't win anything. Do him good. He's got a bit swelled-headed, has Harry. A set-back now and again is good for a swelled head. Don't you think I'm right?'

'I'm sure you are. Where does this Harry Wood live?'

'Seymour Grove, just off the Birkbeck Road. Anybody'll tell you. I can't be sure it's him, but he's not got a car, so he'd have to go by train. I'll check it with Arthur – that's the booking-clerk – when he turns up in the morning. And I hope his kid's come into the world tonight. He's been wrong in his tickets for more than a fortnight with his worries. It's his first, and both him and his wife are nearly forty. So it's been a strain.'

'Will that be all, Superintendent? I've a lot to see to and I'll have to be getting to my duties...'

Littlejohn strolled down the long, dingy road to High Street again. The shops were all closed, but there were lights on in the houses and pubs. There was hardly a soul about. The dismal lighting of the streets made the place look like somewhere in the underworld. Now and then a car passed, driven as though the owner were anxious to get away from it all.

There would probably be another family gathering, an orgy of reproaches and lamentations for the returned James Teasdale. Littlejohn felt he couldn't face it. It was past seven o'clock and he had to arrange for dinner and a place to stay the night. He also wanted to telephone to Cromwell and tell him to enquire from Martha Gomm if Teasdale had, during the past few weeks, encountered someone he knew from Basilden during his tour of fairs. He turned in at the police station.

7

SWEPT FROM HER FEET

T HE BEST HOTEL IN BASILDEN WAS THE SWAN WITH TWO NECKS and the local police had booked a room for Littlejohn there. The dinner was indifferent, but the Superintendent hadn't eaten a proper meal since the one in Ely and he enjoyed it.

'Everythin' to your likin', sir?'

The landlord came and stood by his elbow as he drank his coffee; a little bloated man with a toothbrush of a moustache, who was proud of his guest and had been airing the fact in the bar. His name was Hector Evans and he was locally known as Heck.

'It isn't often we get a Scotland Yard man here,' he told everybody, as he watched his wife serving the drinks. She did most of the work whilst her husband wandered about being sociable.

'Sit down, Mr. Evans, and take a cup of coffee with me.'

'Very nice of you, sir. Don't mind if I do.'

Heck then called for two liqueur brandies.

'On the house, sir. Proud to have you with us.'

He handed Littlejohn a cigar in an aluminium tube. They sat there smoking like a couple of successful business men. Littlejohn's cigar was a dry one and crackled like a lot of old faggots as he smoked it.

'Did you know James Teasdale, Mr. Evans?'

Mr. Evans rolled his cigar to the corner of his mouth and spoke round it.

'Knew him well. He never came here, of course. His wife would have played merry 'ell with him if he'd been seen in a pub. Very different from Little Jimmie. Fancies herself. Big mistake him ever marrying her. He was a nice little chap. I'm sorry about him being murdered. We was by way of being pals. During the war when we had to find work of national importance, Jimmie and me worked in the same shop, testing aeroplane parts.'

'You got to know him well, then?'

'None better. We were in the same shop for nearly three years. Poor Jimmie. He'd have liked to stay on working there, but, of course, when the war ended we became redundant. He'd to go back to his shop and under Mrs. T's thumb again. Working at a factory quite brought him out in those days.'

A long cylinder of ash fell from Heck's cigar and he flailed about dusting it from his clothes.

'Whoever would want to murder an innocent chap like Jimmie...?'

He paused and chuckled.

'Good job his wife can't hear me callin' him Jimmie. She thinks it's common. It's always James this and James that with 'er.'

'Have you been in Basilden long, Mr. Evans?'

'Nearly thirty years. My missus's father... you'll have seen her in the bar... her father was landlord of this place before us. I was a traveller for the brewery, and well... when the old man died, I married Sandra and we settled down in this place.'

Littlejohn could well imagine Heck hanging up his hat.

'You'll know the Teasdales and the Scott-Harris family then.'

'Rather. The major used to be a regular customer here, till he started drinkin' at home. It's bad, that is; drinking alone at home. Old Theo. Scott-Harris always fancied himself off nothing. He'd been an auctioneer in a small way till he married money. Then, he launched out, they tell me. Became a major in the Territorials and started to behave like a real army man. I believe his health's not good now. It's whisky, no doubt, and the wild life he led in his young days.'

'Do you know the Teasdale family well?'

'You mean Jimmie's father and mother. No. They're both dead. As for Jimmie's wife and kids, you should hear my brother-in-law talk about them. Fred Tinker, he's called, and runs the Royal Oak next door to Teasdale's shop.'

'How long has he lived there?'

'Ten years. It's a good house. He could tell you a thing or two about Jimmie's family.'

'I suppose he's told you all there is to tell?'

'Well… We meet regularly after hours. He brings his wife here. Marlene's Sandra's younger sister. Another brandy?'

He didn't wait for an answer but hurried off and returned with two more drinks.

'I thought I'd put 'em in proper balloon glasses. It tastes better, doesn't it? This is good stuff, I can tell you. Some the old man had in for years. Special occasion, wot?'

They smoked in silence for a minute and then Evans spoke.

'Talk about poor Jimmie being murdered. From what my brother-in-law says, it's a wonder *he* didn't murder *her*!'

'You mean Teasdale?'

'Yes. She never left him alone before he took the job of travel-ler. I say traveller because it's what we were all used to calling him. Now, it's come out in the papers that he was some sort of a show-man on a fairground. Fairground! That's a good one. The family'll never get over it.'

Heck then started to laugh until he coughed convulsively. The odd diners at other tables began to turn round to see whatever was the matter with him. He drank from a water jug and composed himself. He pushed his face close to Littlejohn's.

'She never stopped nagging him. You see, they do say she chased Jimmie all over the town till she hooked and married him. Then, she'd big ideas about opening an arts-and-crafts shop. Arts and Crafts! It was a failure from the start.'

Mr. Evans hadn't much to do and he wished to give everybody the impression that he was *persona grata* with the London detective. He spoke slowly and carefully, choosing his words.

'The rows my brother-in-law's heard going on. Not only in the day, but half-way through the night. Not that Jimmie said much. He couldn't get a word in edgeways. When they were first married, she just sat around playing the lady while Jimmie did the housework as well as minding the shop and other things. Then, when the kids began to come, she played the invalid and Jimmie and her sisters looked after her. When the girls grew up, they helped. But from what I hear, Mrs. T. never raised a hand. Sat rocking and reading all day long. She must have driven Jimmie up the wall. No wonder he was happy when he went out to work during the war. And then, after he started travellin', he began to look better again; a new man. As I said, it's a wonder he didn't murder her for the way she treated him.'

The room was small and low-ceilinged, with a few tables with little lamps on them. In one corner, a courting couple were dining, holding hands under the table, and near the fire, a pair of commercial travellers were swopping yarns. The heavy atmosphere and Heck's droning voice made Littlejohn feel sleepy. Come to think of it, he hadn't slept at all last night.

'Once or twice she actually got violent. Threw things at Jimmie...'

'She did?'

'Yes. The walls of the property aren't very thick and my brother-in-law and his wife could often hear the rows that went on.'

'Didn't their daughters interfere?'

'They spend a lot of time out. They mix with what you might call the high society of Basilden, such as it is. Their mother's seen to that. She wants to get 'em off with somebody with money. Make a good match for them. That's why this affair's going to hit her hard. She deserves all that's comin' to her.'

'What were these rows about?'

'From what my brother-in-law overheard, it was always about money. She used to accuse him of asking her to marry him when he knew he couldn't keep her. It seems she had other suitors who'd have let her live like a lady. Who they were, I don't know. She was always at him about what was going to happen to her and the children when Jimmie died, too.'

Littlejohn nodded understandingly. Abuse falling on James Teasdale's head like hailstones. So, he'd gone off and supplemented his income on a game of chance on a fairground whilst his wife was saying he'd got a good job travelling for a big firm in Manchester. And then, he'd met Martha Gomm...

At the inquest in Ely, Martha had appeared to answer a few questions about Teasdale's movements before his death. She had replied quietly and sensibly and had not been harried by the coroner. The police would have quite a lot more to ask her... And all the time, Mrs. Teasdale had behaved as though Martha Gomm didn't exist. She hadn't spoken to her, had refused to meet her, had talked of her as 'my husband's employee'.

'She used to say that she'd been let down.'

Heck's glaucous eyes were fixed on Littlejohn's face. He was enjoying himself.

'What about the daughters?'

'Three fancy pieces! One's engaged to a young doctor in the local hospital. One works for a dentist and the pair of them are out a lot together after hours. The chap's married, too, so how that'll end,

I don't know. The other's knocking round with a bookie. Her ma doesn't much fancy that, but as he's in the money, she's probably disposed to overlook his other shortcomings...'

Littlejohn rose and stretched himself.

'I'd better be getting along. I've some matters to attend to before I go to bed. I'll see you later.'

The landlord was reluctant to let him go, but agreed.

'A day and night job, the police, isn't it?'

He gave Littlejohn another cigar like a small torpedo and saw him to the door.

Only half the face of the church clock was illuminated, but Littlejohn could make out that it was half-past nine. Perhaps the sharp edge of the family reunion in High Street would have worn off. He made his way down the rows of shops to the Teasdale home.

It was raining. A thin mist of rain which clung to the clothes and formed a halo round the shabby electric lights of the road. The town square was almost deserted. There were lights on in the church and the choir were practising. The music of their anthem mingled with that of a pub across the way where the patrons were singing to the accompaniment of an old piano.

Littlejohn rang the bell at the side of the shop door. Footsteps across the floor and someone fumbled with the lock. The door opened slightly on the end of a chain.

'Who is it?'

'Littlejohn.'

It was Chloe, Mrs. Teasdale's sister, the olde-tyme dancer.

'The rest have gone to make some arrangements for the funeral, the day after tomorrow. I'm just sitting with my sister till the girls come home. They're at the dressmaker's about the mourning. Come inside.'

The lamp from the back quarters made a tunnel of light through the darkness of the shop. The living-room was hot and stuffy and the smell of cigar smoke hung about from the efforts of the corn-chandler, now gone to his club to discuss the family news and, probably, to contradict some of the unsavoury items spread abroad by the evening papers.

Mrs. Teasdale was sitting in the usual rocking-chair idling the time away and her sister must have been clearing up the remnants of family refreshment when Littlejohn rang. There were soiled cups and saucers on the dining-table, plates bearing crumbs of bread and cake, biscuits on another plate and, in the middle of the lot, a large heavy-looking plum-cake ornamented with marzipan and icing.

The murder had evidently not destroyed anybody's appetite.

Mrs. Teasdale didn't rise. She didn't even stop rocking; but by a slight stiffening of the body, changed gear and modified the pace of her to-ing and fro-ing.

'Excuse my late call, but I came to ask if there was anything more I could do to help, Mrs. Teasdale.'

The face of the newly made widow lengthened as her expression changed from lazy almost voluptuous comfort to one of simulated grief.

'How kind of you. No. I don't think there is anything more just now, Superintendent. My family have gathered round to support me and have been a great help.'

Chloe scuttered in and out, gathering the wreckage of the feast and removing it to the kitchen behind. Now and then she cast an almost coy look on Littlejohn.

'Please sit down. A cup of tea or a little refreshment…?'

Chloe paused in her labours, apologetic, almost distressed at having carried off the feast under what might be the nose of a hungry man.

'I'm so sorry. I hadn't thought. The upset, you know...'

'I've just dined, thank you. I don't wish to disturb you.'

Mrs. Teasdale smiled sadly.

'Those who have nothing to hide are not easily disturbed.'

Was there some hint, some suspicion concerning her husband and his recent behaviour in the words?

'Will you take a little of something, Mr. Littlejohn?'

There was a plated tray on the sideboard with two used glasses and another clean one surrounding a bottle of whisky. It had obviously recently been used by the brothers-in-law. Mrs. Teasdale indicated that Littlejohn might help himself, but he declined. There was only a tablespoonful remaining in the bottle.

What struck Littlejohn most was the absence of the usual atmosphere of mourning around the place. They couldn't, of course, on account of the shop, have the body there, but there is usually about the home of the dead an ante-funeral atmosphere, a restraint caused by grief, a sense of depression. There was none here. Instead, Mrs. Teasdale looked very placid and comfortable and her sister was almost gay. It was only when Chloe leaned near him to remove the heavyweight cake and panted a little from her efforts that the truth dawned upon him. He received a light blast of gin from her breath.

The pair of them had been taking a little something on the sly to keep up their spirits.

Littlejohn looked across at the woman in the rocking-chair.

The thin lips, the two deep lines between the corners of the mouth and the nose, the narrow nostrils, the shallow forehead and untidy grey hair. Discontent and pride written all over the face. And disappointment in the nondescript washed-out blue eyes in their pouched sockets and faded lids.

She had accused Teasdale of asking her to marry him when he knew he couldn't keep her.

Tomorrow, when callers came with condolences, and the day after when, dressed in black from head to foot, she followed the coffin, she'd assume an injured but dignified pose, the way a lady would behave. The lady she thought Teasdale had prevented her from becoming.

'If you are still here the day after tomorrow, Superintendent, I would like you to be present at the funeral...'

She said it *à propos* of nothing at all, and Littlejohn said he would do his best to be there.

'It will be a large gathering, I expect. Our family is greatly respected in the town.'

She slurred her words slightly. Littlejohn could imagine the sympathetic Chloe urging her to take a drink or two for the sake of her nerves, and she'd probably overdone it.

'You were born here?'

'Yes. My mother was the daughter of a large millowner, a very respected family...'

'And your father, the major, he also was a native of these parts?'

'Yes. A J.P., too, until his retirement. He has many friends here. The funeral will be a great tribute and a great comfort.'

She sighed. Never a word about the late James Teasdale. He'd blotted his family copybook with a vengeance. He didn't enter into the matter at all. The failure, the no-account, who'd made a mess of everything he'd ever tried to do, and fetched up running a hoop-la stall on fairgrounds.

'You were married young, Mrs. Teasdale?'

She raised herself from the lounging posture and suddenly took the offensive.

'I was too young. Swept from my feet. I was inexperienced. One ought not to marry on impulse, but be sure that the partner one takes is able to keep one in the way one has been accustomed to...'

She seemed to know what she wished to say. In fact she'd learned it by heart, but was finding it difficult to put the words in order.

In the kitchen, sounds of washing-up. Chloe was dealing with the supper dishes and couldn't hear the diatribe. Otherwise she might have intervened.

'My father advised me against the marriage, but I was headstrong. One is headstrong when one's young and inexperienced. I have paid for it.'

She shed a few tears.

'Excuse me. I'm very upset by recent events. I don't quite know what I'm going to do, Superintendent. You are very kind and I feel I can confide in you. In short, I shall be dependent on my children for my very bread and butter.'

Instead of weeping, this time, she looked annoyed.

'He probably hasn't left me a penny. I cannot tell you what I've put up with in married life. First of all, the shop, trying to sell things which nobody wanted. After we married, he confessed that he had only saved one hundred pounds. We had to borrow money to buy the stock. He started painting pictures. That didn't last long. There is a limit to pictures in a town like this. I'm sure many of our friends and relations bought James's pictures out of pity. Their houses must have been filled with pictures they didn't want. It was humiliating! Degrading...!'

She was going full steam ahead now. Littlejohn wondered whether or not the washing-up would end before the confessions.

'Then, as the pictures fell off, he took to repairing bicycles. He said he'd once been a cyclist. Imagine it! Bicycles! The cellars were littered with wheels, chains, tyres, and three-speed gears! It meant I had to look after the shop. A thing I'd never been used to. And then, the children began to arrive... The strain broke me down. I was an invalid for a long time. Three children in four years. It wasn't good enough!'

'What wasn't good enough, dear?'

Chloe, smiling after a job well done, appeared and heard the tail-end of the lamentations.

'It wasn't good enough, James giving me three daughters in four years. I was just telling the Superintendent that...'

She dried up. She'd lost the train of her thoughts.

'It doesn't matter. But I'm glad Mr. Littlejohn called. I want to ask you something, Superintendent. Now, please answer me frankly. I can bear it. I'm used to the indignities he had heaped upon me since our marriage...'

She paused to take breath.

'Was the woman in court, the common gipsy-looking woman... was she... was she...'

Chloe bent and put her arms round her sister.

'Don't, Elvira. Don't. You've been through enough...'

'Leave me alone! I insist on knowing. Was the woman James's mistress? I knew he was unfaithful to me. I've known for a long time.'

Chloe interrupted again.

'How can you say such a thing? You've never known it at all. It's not true. It's not true, is it, Superintendent?'

'I don't know, Mrs. Cornford. I must admit that he had a woman helping him with his hoop-la...'

Mrs. Teasdale shuddered and her teeth chattered at the very name.

'... She helped him, particularly looking after the business when he came here at week-ends.'

'She was his mistress! I know it! I knew he was spending his money on someone else. We, hardly able to keep body and soul together, and he... It was wicked...'

She stopped dead.

'I shan't go to the funeral.'

Littlejohn said he'd better be going, as he hadn't had any sleep the night before on account of the journey. He urged Mrs. Teasdale to retire as well, as she hadn't slept either.

'I shan't go to bed and I shan't go to the funeral. I couldn't even pay my respects to such a deceiver and seducer...'

He let himself out, leaving the two women arguing about it.

Funeral! Divorce! Adulterer! Street-Woman! The words were flying round his ears like bullets when he closed the door of the dark shop, which smelled of paint, turpentine, cheap cigars, sackcloth, and stale leather.

Outside, the streets were empty. The last bus was passing the door, the Royal Oak was closed and there were shadows, cleaning up, on the opaque windows. The fish-and-chip shop at the end of the block was almost empty, emitting a hot smell of stale cooking fat. The only figure in the deserted square was a solitary drunk, offering to fight anybody who would take him on.

8

TALK OF DIVORCE

AFTER SEEING OFF LITTLEJOHN FROM ELY, CROMWELL MADE his way to Tylecote. The day was fine and a breeze had sprung up. The floods were falling and at almost every house along the route, women were drying out their belongings and men shovelling the mud and refuse from their houses and gardens.

He reached Tylecote at three o'clock. People were working like ants in the village street, tidying up or exchanging experiences about the damage. There had been no school and the children were enjoying themselves, slopping about in the water in gumboots. Some even had bare feet and were paddling; others were sailing boats in the shallows.

Cromwell found Martha Gomm was living in Tylecote still and assisting her landlady to clean and dry out carpets and rugs and swill out the silt from the downstairs rooms. Mrs. Southery was in a highly nervous state. She confided to Cromwell that she didn't know what she'd have done without Martha Gomm.

'She's forgot her own troubles and taken on mine. Never will I say a wrong word about her nor listen to one, either.'

Cromwell was wearing a cloth cap. It seemed more appropriate in the circumstances than the bowler hat in which he usually did his work. He looked free and easy and Mrs. Southery took to him at once. He gave her a hand moving furniture about and carrying buckets here and there.

'Did you know the pair of them weren't married?'

'Not till they found him dead. If I'd known and turned them

out, I'd never have forgiven myself. A girl like Martha is good for any man, wedded or not.'

'Where is she?'

'She's at my sister's in Fetting, two miles along the road. My sister's house is on dry ground; it's higher than here. Martha's gone to get some bedding. Everything feels damp, even if the water hasn't touched it... I don't know however I'll get over this.'

'We'll soon fix you up. A good cleaning up and some warm fires and you won't know it's happening.'

Mrs. Southery expressed her doubts, but didn't argue. They were too busy. Cromwell was smoking his pipe and cleaning the bare boards of the living-room with a mop and a bucket of hot water.

'She's here now...'

Martha Gomm was pushing an old bicycle along the garden path. There was a huge bundle tied on the carrier and she held another under her arm. Mrs. Southery introduced her to Cromwell.

'He's a friend of Mr. Littlejohn's.'

Martha's cheeks were flushed from her exertions, which she seemed to be carrying out without much interest. She moved like something automatic. She looked at the room and then cast a grateful glance at Cromwell.

'Thanks.'

Mrs. Southery went upstairs to unpack the clean bedding and left the two of them together.

Martha's hair still hung long and lank, framing her pale oval face. She looked tired out from labour and grief and only held herself upright with difficulty.

'Sit down and talk to me, Miss Gomm. Where's the tea things? I'll make some.'

Cromwell carried on with the job in spite of her resistance, finding the necessary things and spreading them on the bare boards of the table. She had brought in, along with the rest of the stuff, a biscuit tin filled with provisions and took out scones and butter and added them to the drinks. Then she laid a tray for Mrs. Southery and took it upstairs to her. Cromwell waited for her to return and then they sat together. They ate and drank in silence for a minute or two.

'Feel like talking to me a bit?'

She gave him a friendly look. After all, he had almost alone created some order out of the place, which was now quite homely again, in spite of the bare floors.

Dusk was falling. Outside there was a chatter of voices, pails rattling, water swishing about. The local volunteer firemen were operating a small pump to get rid of the water in the low-lying places. They seemed quite jolly about it now that the rain had ceased. One was keeping up his morale by shrill whistling.

'It's getting dark. We'll have to bring in the carpets and things off the clothes lines as soon as we've finished tea.'

'Have you any idea who might have wanted to kill Mr. Teasdale?'

She looked at him blankly for a moment and he corrected himself.

'I mean Mr. Lane...'

'No.'

She ate a scone listlessly and passed him the plate, inviting him to help himself.

'He'd no enemies here or among the fairground fraternity?'

'No. Everybody liked him. He was cheerful and ready to give anybody a hand. Perhaps it was his bein' so small, too, among so many big men on the fairs made them always ready to help him. Some of them seemed to treat him like a boy. They even defended him against the bullies who came along. I know what a lot of them would want to do to whoever killed him.'

She didn't seem sorry for herself at all, nor did she show any sign of tears. All the pity she had was for the little man, her companion, whom someone had killed.

'It was wanton. That's what it was. Wanton, to kill a man like James.'

'How did you get mixed up with the fairground business?'

'My parents died and I lived with a stepsister of my father's till I couldn't stand it any more. I stuck it till I was sixteen and then I left them. They'd got me a job in a glove factory which closed down, and when I was out of work my aunt kept taunting me with being an expense to them. I ended up as a sort of waitress in an hotel near Brightlingsea and while I was there, I met my husband. He was with the fair. I fell for him and he invited me to join him and live in his caravan. I said not unless he married me, which he did. I told the rest to Mr. Littlejohn. Do you want to know, too?'

'No, he told me about you. Your husband died, didn't he?'

'Yes... Hadn't we better be getting in the things from the garden? It'll be damp out there at dusk.'

They hauled in the heavy carpets and rugs and the rest of the paraphernalia. They were all still damp and they stowed them in the scullery. Now and then, Cromwell added another question.

'Do you know that James Lane wasn't killed here?'

'What do you mean? His body was found in the river.'

She stopped at her work and stood facing him, her hands on her hips, her large eyes questioning.

'He was murdered somewhere else and brought here. Why would anybody do that? Why not leave him wherever the crime was committed?'

'That's an easy one. It was to make it look as if I did it. As if we'd had a row and I'd killed him. Somebody must have mistaken me for a gipsy or something and thought I was up to their tricks. Or the tricks people say gipsies do. Personally, all the gipsies I've met at fairs are very decent. They'd never think of shedding blood. I didn't kill James. I'm not that sort. Specially with a man like James. If he'd wanted to get rid of me, he'd only to say so and I'd have gone. But he didn't.'

They went on with their work. She seemed to be thinking hard as they folded the carpets.

'How do you know he didn't die here?'

'Medical evidence. To put it simply, he died before he'd had time to digest the tea he ate at Basilden.'

She nodded.

'I thought so. He said when he left, that he'd telephone me from Basilden and ask how things were in Tylecote. If there wasn't going to be a fair, we'd make arrangements and perhaps meet somewhere else. He never rang me up. He was to telephone the police station three doors away and ask Clifton to bring me to the 'phone. He didn't do it. He wasn't one for going back on his arrangements.'

They finished their work and returned for another cup of tea. Upstairs, Mrs. Southery was still busy in the bedrooms, bumping the furniture and throwing things about.

'Did Lane ever talk of marrying you?'

She put down her teacup.

'Sometimes. He said if he could persuade his wife to divorce him, we'd get married. He said he'd feel more settled and he wanted always to be with me. He'd got tired of going up north every week to keep up what he called the deception.'

'When did he say that?'

'A time or two, but it always ended in us talking about his family and how it might affect the future of the girls. I told him often enough that I was content with things as they were.'

'But he wasn't? He liked this life better.'

'He said he did.'

'When was the divorce last mentioned?'

'Before he left me last week-end.'

'What did he say?'

'He said his wife was getting suspicious, he thought. He hadn't said anything to her, nor had she. But he felt somehow she was always watching him and one day it would all come out. I asked him not to tell her himself. If she was thinking things, I said, he'd better let her speak of it.'

'And he promised?'

'He said he'd leave it for the time being, but that, sooner or later, he'd got to have a showdown. He was coming round to the idea that the girls were settled and that if his wife divorced *him*, she'd come out of it all right. In fact, he said, people would pity her and sympathise with her and that was what would suit her.'

'You'd have married him?'

'It would have been nice to be settled down with a man like James. But what's the use of talking about it now?'

She rose and quickly gathered the tea things and took them in the scullery. He could hear her beginning to wash up and went to join her.

'I'll wipe the dishes.'

She smiled for the first time.

'Quite domesticated, aren't you? Have you any family?'

He told her about his wife and girls and about Littlejohn and how much he enjoyed his work.

'Did Lane ever say what his wife would do, if he told her about you?'

'He said she'd probably refuse to divorce him just out of sheer spite. Even if he paid her good alimony, it wouldn't change her mind. They weren't happy, but the thought of him finding happiness elsewhere would make her more determined than ever to oppose it. She despised him, he told me, but she wouldn't release him on any account.'

'What then?'

'Well, he said, in that case, he'd just stop going home. Just send her the money, but not make the trips north.'

'Was all this his talk lately?'

'Yes. He'd only started to get properly fed up with the situation over the past few weeks.'

'Why?'

She took the towel from him, straightened it, and hung it to dry over a wooden rail near the sink. She was evidently making up her mind about something and Cromwell guessed before she spoke.

'Is there a baby on the way?'

She didn't move a muscle or even blush. She just stood there, patting the sodden towel into shape.

'Yes.'

'When?'

'Oh… next Spring.'

'Did he know?'

'I told him. I couldn't do anything else. I'm not one for keeping my own counsel with a man like James. I'm not sorry. Even now, I'm not sorry. He's left me something to remember him by. I have to look at it that way.'

'What did he say?'

'He was glad. It might have been his first. He said that settled it. He'd get his freedom some way and we'd be married. He said a fairground was no place to bring up a baby. We'd give it up and buy a shop.'

Another shop! Poor Jim Lane! Not content with making a complete mess of one attempt at running a shop of all sorts, he was now planning to start another.

'I know what you're thinking. About his misery in his other shop. But this time he'd have had me with him and I wouldn't have let him down or despised him. We'd have made a go of it.'

Somehow, Cromwell's co-operation in her duties had brought them together, created an understanding. He was sitting on a chair in the middle of the floor and she was leaning against the sink, her hands on either side of her gripping the rim. They might have been old friends, and there was interest and vitality about her again.

'And that made him want to make a fresh start and cut away from his old life?'

'Yes.'

'And you think he was seeking an opportunity of telling his wife and getting a divorce.'

'Not exactly. You've no need to think he told her last week-end when he was home. He promised me he wouldn't until I said he could. I even told him we could go on as we were. After all, I've lived among this sort of thing half my life. People don't bother about illegitimate children like they used to do. The child would have his father with him... or her... and that was something. Half the kids of that kind you meet at fairs, don't even know who their fathers are. Their mothers don't know, many a time, either. But this was different. I was content if he kept on going north, but came back to us. But he wouldn't have it. He was sure it would be a boy and he swore it should have a better chance than he had. Now, I don't know about all that. I don't even think about it.'

'You're sure he didn't speak of this when he was last at home?'

'Quite sure. Before he left me for the last time, I just said to him, "Remember, you promised not to say anything yet". He promised again, but he was getting impatient about it. I said he could tell his wife when we'd settled what we were going to do in the future, and not before.'

'Did anyone else know of all this?'

'No. I didn't want anybody to know until we'd got everything decided properly. I don't know why I've told you. But you've been so decent about everything and it's easier to talk to you about these things than to Mr. Littlejohn. You see, he didn't help me with the washing up...'

She actually laughed, as though, for a moment, she'd forgotten her plight and her grief and returned to the normal things of life for a brief time.

'Oh, if he'd wiped the dishes for you, you'd have found him just as easy to talk with. He's one of the best.'

'I know he is. He was very kind to me, but you didn't expect me to start telling him about babies with everybody rushing in and out and the floods running in at the front door. You've caught me at the right moment...'

To have someone sympathetic to talk to seemed to have lightened her spirits considerably.

'What are you going to do now, Miss Gomm?'

'Martha's the name, please. You are my friend.'

'Yes. Well, Martha, what next?'

'He even thought of that. We won a thousand pounds once on the pools. He opened a banking account for me in the Post Office. We always filled in a pools coupon every week, but that was the only time we had any real luck. I didn't want him to put it in my name, but he insisted. We were partners in the business and there it is. There's over a thousand pounds in it now. That will see me through.'

'You know he had a banking account of his own with a fair sum in it?'

'Yes. He did well on the fairs. He wasn't the fairground kind, and that somehow attracted people. They were even waiting for us to turn up at some of the fairs. He was greeted like an old friend and people used to come and take a hand at the hoop-la just for the sake of seeing him and having a word with him. He was a witty sort and used to cheer people up.'

Very different from the James Teasdale of Basilden, from all accounts. A failure, a dud. His new life must have suited him. And now, that happiness was just round the corner, someone had...

Cromwell put on his coat and offered his hand to Martha Gomm.

'Well, Martha, good-bye for the present. I must get back to Ely. I've booked a room there and I'm off north to meet the chief in Basilden tomorrow. I'll have to tell him what you've told me. You won't mind?'

'No. And thank you for the help you've given us. You wipe dishes very nicely.'

'I'm properly trained. I'll see you in a day or two.'

He bade Mrs. Southery good-bye, too, put on his cap and rain-coat, and made for the road where his car was parked.

Clifton, the policeman, was waiting for him. He saluted dutifully.

'So, there you are, sir. I've been waitin' for you.'

He handed Cromwell a grubby piece of paper.

'We dried out the car that Lane came in and we found that in one corner of the pocket. It was a bit soggy, but you can just read it. It's nothing much, but might be of interest.'

'Thank you, Clifton. What is it?'

He switched on the headlamps and examined the bobby's find in the light of them.

Thrutchley's Garage. Basilden.
Always Open.

A settled bill for 8 gallons of petrol and a quart of oil, dated the night James Teasdale died.

9

BARBARA, IRENE, AND CHRIS

CROMWELL HAD TELEPHONED FROM ELY EARLY IN THE MORN-ing to say that he was on his way to Basilden. Littlejohn could hardly wait for him to arrive. It was almost like being in a foreign country and with his old colleague there to support him and discuss the case with him, things would be much better.

He had spent the night at the Swan with Two Necks. They had a comfortable room or two and he reserved one for Cromwell, who was due to arrive that night. The landlord hung about as Littlejohn ate his breakfast. To prevent his intrusion, Littlejohn propped the morning paper against the jampot on the table and read it. He found himself in the headlines. Heck was obviously eager to talk about it.

'See you're in the heavy type this morning, Super,' he'd said as soon as Littlejohn entered the dining-room. Then, fortunately, the beer had arrived from the brewery and he'd been called away.

It was fine, but Basilden was under heavy clouds, which gave everything a drab, dreary look. The shops in the square were open-ing and people were passing on their ways to work. Boxes of fish were appearing at a shop almost opposite and the greengrocer two doors away had just arrived with his lorry full of new vegetables and fruit.

The case was now centring entirely on Basilden. Teasdale had been killed not long after eating his evening meal. Then, his mur-derer had very likely loaded the body in Teasdale's own car and taken it to where it should have been next morning, near Ely. Why?

The answer seemed simple. The murderer had wished to divert attention from Basilden and transfer it to the place where Teasdale would appear next day. The suspects would then be Martha Gomm or some of Little Jim's fairground associates. In the diary found in the dead man's pocket, he'd written details of his fairground visits and the murderer could have found out almost the exact location of Teasdale's next port of call.

But the murderer had forgotten one thing. The condition of the victim's stomach. Quite understandable; quite easily overlooked by an amateur.

The whole affair boiled down to the family, including old Scott-Harris, or some unknown enemy of Teasdale's who'd not yet turned up. There was also Harry Wood, the singer, to be investigated. He'd been at Norwich at the time Teasdale and Martha Gomm had been at the fair in Lowestoft. Perhaps he'd taken a trip to the sea and met them. It might be a mare's nest. On the other hand, Wood might have encountered Teasdale there.

Littlejohn glanced at the newspaper again.

FLOOD MURDER. SCOTLAND YARD ON THE CASE
Superintendent Littlejohn Visits Basilden.

He was sharing the headlines with a couple who'd eloped.

SALOME GRIERSON MADE WARD OF THE COURT
Father Weeps as He Pursues Fleeing Couple to Scotland.

He put on his hat and coat and went into the town square. The policeman on point duty saluted smartly as he passed and the loafers outside the labour exchange paused in their grousing about current conditions to point him out to one another.

Teasdale's shop was closed and the large dark-blue blind of the window was drawn. On the door, a card stuck down with gelatine lozenges. *Closed owing to Bereavement.* Littlejohn rang the bell on the door-jamb and could hear it whirring somewhere in the interior.

Barbara opened the door, just as the town clock chimed a quarter to ten. She seemed surprised to see the Superintendent at that hour. She wasn't properly dressed and wore a flowered wrapper over her underclothes, showing an expanse of white bosom when she moved and it gaped open. Her hair was bound in a large headcloth.

'Good morning, Superintendent. You're an early bird. Come in...'
She stood aside to admit him to the dark shop.

'You'll have to excuse us. We're all at sixes and sevens. We stayed up late and didn't get up till nine. Mother's still in bed. She's feeling the strain. After you left last night, she collapsed.'

She led the way to the living quarters. It was brighter there. The curtains had been drawn and the daylight made the room seem more depressing than ever. Littlejohn realised that he hadn't seen it in full daylight before. The place was situated pleasantly enough. Beyond the window there was a spacious courtyard, mainly cobblestoned and a bit shabby-looking. In one corner, the remains of a neglected garden, with a tumbledown summerhouse. Then some dilapidated outbuildings which might once have been a stable. The yard was entered through a large gate beside which stood a wooden shed, presumably Teasdale's garage.

The room was more untidy than ever. The remains of a breakfast still on the table. Measured by the relics of the meal, bereavement hadn't impaired the appetites of the three people who'd recently eaten. The menu, judging from the leavings, had probably been cereals, bacon and eggs, marmalade, and tea from a huge pot standing in the middle of the wreckage.

'We've only just finished breakfast.'

Barbara lolled about in her usual lazy way. She had no make-up on, but her clear complexion didn't seem to need much. There were dark patches of fatigue under her eyes.

'Irene and Christine are both off work today. They're upstairs dressing.'

Littlejohn could imagine it, judging from the voices and tramping feet on the floor above. Then Irene descended upon them. She seemed surprised, too, at the early visit.

'You're an early bird, Superintendent.'

Again! Littlejohn wondered at what time the Teasdale ménage got going under normal conditions.

'I won't keep you long. I just called to get a little more information about the movements of everyone on the night your father died.'

Footsteps overhead moved in the direction of the stairs, reached by a door in the corner of the room, and then paused, as though someone were listening. Christine shouted down.

'Who's there?'

Irene called back up the stairs.

'Superintendent Littlejohn, Chris.'

'Early bird!'

Nothing much original about the Teasdales' metaphors! Chris hurried down. She and Irene were both fully dressed and Irene was showing some uneasiness about Barbara's *deshabille*. She hurried to her, and hastily arranged the wrapper to show a little less of her throat and chest.

The three girls all stood around, waiting for Littlejohn to speak.

'Who's there?'

Now it was Mrs. Teasdale calling in a feeble voice! Irene shouted from the bottom of the stairs.

'It's the Superintendent, Mother. No need to worry. He doesn't need you...'

'You don't, do you, Superintendent?'

'No, thanks.'

'He says he doesn't need you, Mother.'

'What?'

'He says you needn't disturb yourself.'

'He's an early caller, isn't he?'

Irene didn't reply and Mrs. Teasdale subsided.

'I called to ask where you all were when your father left home on the night he died.'

The door-bell rang again. Irene, the active one, dressed in a becoming navy-blue costume, answered. It was the milkman and she returned carrying three bottles which she put on the table among the rest of the litter.

'You'll excuse the mess the house is in, Superintendent. We're all at sixes and sevens.'

'That's understandable, Miss Teasdale. I'll just make a note of where you all were and leave you. I'm sorry to intrude, but it's rather important. Mere routine, though. Don't upset your mother about it.'

Christine, who hadn't said a word except good morning to Littlejohn, disappeared into the unknown parts behind the living-room.

Barbara was sitting rocking in her mother's armchair. At fifty she'd be a replica of her mother; lazy, slovenly, easy-going.

Irene was anxious to get the business done and get Littlejohn out of the place. She was obviously ashamed of his finding it so untidy.

'I'll do what I can to help.'

'Your father and mother were here at seven o'clock, I believe, and then your father left.'

'Yes. That's what Mother said. They were in alone. We'd all said good-bye to Father and gone out.'

'First then, Miss Barbara.'

Barbara stopped rocking and answered after Irene had again hitched up her wrapper to restore decency.

'I was in Halstone. Alex had the day free and we went to the Blue Boar for a meal. We left here about four. I said good-bye to Dad then.'

Irene had, she said, gone to church, which started at six-thirty. She'd said good-bye and left at six-fifteen.

As Littlejohn wrote it down in his book, he felt a bit puzzled about Irene's choice of boyfriend. A bookie, they'd told him. He must have been a man of good taste, for Irene seemed by far the best of the bunch.

Christine was back to answer her questions.

'A party of us went out by road to Exelby, a few miles from here. We stayed at the Unicorn there for tea and didn't start off back till just after seven. We had a few drinks... Father had gone when I returned. It was around nine. I just called to leave a note for Mother that I'd be in late and not to wait up, and then went out again.'

Alex would, of course, confirm Barbara's statement; the parson himself, if needs be, could support Irene's; and Harry, the dentist, had driven Christine to the Unicorn.

'Your father and mother were alone, then, when it came time for him to go?'

'Yes.'

All the aunts and uncles were churchgoers and weren't, therefore, likely to call until after service. Irene was emphatic about it.

'Uncle Sam's a deacon of Bethesda and it was the anniversary service. Nothing would keep him away. And Auntie Chloe and Uncle Walter were going, too. As for Uncle Bertram, he's organist at St. Chad's, where I attend. He was there, as usual.'

Littlejohn could imagine the glowing-nosed Bertram at the keyboard!

'What time did you get home, Miss Irene?'

'Eight o'clock. After service. I'd arranged to meet Joe, that's my friend, at eight-thirty. I called to tidy up.'

'Was your mother here?'

'No. She'd gone to see Grandfather. She always calls there to see him and stays to supper with him on Sunday evenings.'

'What time did she get home?'

'I don't know exactly. I got in after eleven and found she'd gone to bed. She was asleep and I didn't disturb her.'

'Was she back when you called in around nine, Miss Christine?'

'No. The place was in darkness. I left almost right away.'

'So you all were out late. You found her in bed and asleep when you got in?'

The three of them agreed.

Littlejohn thanked them and excused himself. By the time he'd reached the shop door he could hear them chattering excitedly together.

The landlord of the hotel next door was leaning against the doorpost, smoking, enjoying the air, and watching the passers-by.

'Morning,' he said.

Littlejohn returned his greeting and asked him where Thrutchley's Garage could be found. Cromwell had mentioned the invoice for petrol over the telephone.

'Round the corner. First to the right. Bit of a corker, this murder of Teasdale, isn't it? I'd never have believed it. Such a nice chap. Sure he didn't commit suicide? I wouldn't blame him.'

'Why?'

'Family led him a dog's life. My brother-in-law at the Swan, where you're stayin', told me you'd been inquiring about 'em. They thought themselves a cut above poor old Jim and didn't hesitate to let 'im know it.'

Mr. Tinker lit another cigarette from the stub of the last one, and flung the fag-end far into the road. A small man, with a curl plastered over his forehead. He looked a bit like a caricature of Disraeli, except that he had a moustache.

'It used to disgust me.'

He spat accurately into the road this time.

'What time did he leave home last Sunday night, do you know, Mr. Tinker?'

'As near seven as dammit. I know it was about seven, because I'd been listening to a favourite programme on the wireless and when it was over, at seven, I went in the courtyard at the back for a breath of air. We share the same courtyard, but have separate gates and outbuildings. Well, Jim was just gettin' out his car and it took a bit of startin'. It was a real old crock and he always had trouble that way when it had been standin' a bit. He got it to go as I was there and drove off. His missus was with him. He used to take her to her father's before he went on his trip on Sunday nights.'

'Did you see Mrs. Teasdale return afterwards?'

'No. But I heard her. She got back about a quarter to eleven. I heard her bumpin' about next door. The walls aren't so thick and we can hear most of what goes on.'

'Is that the time she usually gets back?'

'No. It's generally about ten. She was later than usual.'

'You're sure about the time?'

'Pretty well. We close at half-past ten and I'd just tidied up. It takes round a quarter hour. She went to bed right away, too. I went on the front for a breath of fresh air and the light was on in her bedroom. She sleeps on the front.'

Mr. Tinker, the fresh-air fiend, thereupon lit another cigarette.

That was about all; so Littlejohn left him.

Thrutchley's Garage was little better than a shanty erected on a piece of waste ground at the end of a row of houses. There were two pumps in front and a yard full of tumbledown old cars at the side. Mr. Thrutchley – for he answered to his name eagerly – was lying under an old crock parked in the interior, his feet alone showing. On hearing he was needed, Mr. Thrutchley, judging from the movement of the feet, turned over on his stomach under the vehicle and arrived in front of Littlejohn crawling like a large slug.

He was a fat, flabby man dressed in oily overalls, wore a greasy cloth cap to hide his almost total baldness, had a button nose, and talked in a shrill, feminine voice completely out of keeping with his huge body.

'What can I do for you, sir?' he fluted.

'Did Mr. Teasdale call here for petrol last Sunday night, Mr. Thrutchley?'

'I don't know. I weren't on duty. I'm a bellringer at parish church and I've never missed a ring on Sundays, except wakes, when I go on my holidays to Scarborough, for past twenty years. But our Granville was in charge of garage. He'll know. Granville!!!'

Littlejohn wasn't aware that there was anyone in the place except Mr. Thrutchley and a boy apprentice, who had been standing by with open mouth ever since he arrived. Granville Thrutchley had, like his parent, been silently meditating on his back under an old car, and on hearing his name, shouted from his hiding place in a voice as shrill as his father's.

'Wot, Dad?'

'Come 'ere.'

Nothing was visible of Granville but the soles of his shoes, which needed repairing, and these reversed as Granville turned on his belly to creep into the light of day. He emerged, a long youth, undulating like a snake, as thin as his dad was fat, big-nosed, with a calf-lick over one eye and prominent large teeth. He must have taken after his mother.

'Wot?'

'Gentleman wants to know if Jimmy Teasdale called 'ere for petrol night he were murdered.'

'What for?'

Littlejohn explained and introduced himself.

'Oh. You're the man from Scotland Yard. I read about you in the papers this mornin'. Nice job *you've* got. What were you askin'? Did Jimmy call here on Sunday night? Yes, he did. He called for eight gallons o' petrol and some oil.'

'What time?'

'What time? Seven o'clock. Church clock'd just struck.'

'Was anybody with him?'

'Was anybody with him? Yes; his missis. She was givin' him what-for, too, I can tell you. I say, she was givin' him what-for.'

This constant repetition of Granville's got on one's nerves in time, especially as his shrill voice echoed round the neighbourhood. It was as if Littlejohn were not questioning him loudly enough for all to hear, and he was forced to echo it all like an amplifier.

'What do you mean by "what-for"?'

'What do I mean? I mean she was naggin' him something awful.'

'What about?'

'Wot about? How should I know what about? The row 'ad started before they got 'ere.'

Mr. Thrutchley, senior, here thought it right to intervene and rebuke Granville, whose truculence displeased him.

'Now, Granville, just keep a civil tongue in your 'ead with the Superintendent. Speak civil. You never know when you might need the police yourself.'

And he turned to Littlejohn to apologise and explain for the lack of good manners of his offspring.

'He's been a bit difficult since he were a lad, when he fell off a ladder on his head,' he said *sotto voce*, which could be heard by all the crowd attracted to the garage by the noise.

Granville expressed contrition and explained the reason.

'Ah can't stand Mrs. Teasdale. I bet she murdered him herself. Ah say...'

'They were quarrelling when they arrived here?'

'They were that.'

'Did you hear what was said, Granville?'

'I couldn't tell half wot was said, because she was crying and sobbin' and carryin' on like someone with hysterics.'

'What did you hear her say?'

Littlejohn waited for the echo, but it didn't come this time.

'She'd always been a good wife to him. Which wasn't true, because I know, as well as anybody else, how bad she treated him.'

'Anything else?'

'She was talkin' all the time and sobbin' somethin' awful. The engine of Jimmy's old car made such a noise, you couldn't hear yourself speak, and when he shut it off as I put petrol in, Jimmy turned on her and told 'er to shut up in front of other people. And *then* she said she wouldn't shut up, and that started a row about shutting up and not shutting up. Then he started the engine again and I couldn't hear the rest. I do know that she said she'd never, never agree to it. Wot she wasn't goin' to agree to, I couldn't make out...'

Mr. Thrutchley, senior, thereupon raised a grubby paw in front of junior's face to indicate it was time he shut up, too.

'What direction did they move off in?'

'They always went to old Scott-Harris's on Sundays. I expect they went there then.'

'Well, thank you for your help.'

'Don't mention it.'

Granville thereupon returned to his work, and disappeared under the old car like a worm going to ground. His father followed suit only with more dignity, and the open-mouthed boy having vanished in the darkness of the garage, Littlejohn found himself alone with the old cars.

THE EMPTY ROOM

T HE SCOTT-HARRIS HOUSE LOOKED EVEN MORE FORMIDABLE
in the daylight. The surrounding trees, mere shadows when
Littlejohn had last seen them by night, were now revealed as old,
neglected poplars with black trunks and knotted leafless branches.
The soil under them was black and sour and covered by the
decayed mould of last autumn, with menacing-looking fungus
springing up among it. The gravel drive was sprouting long grass
and the iron railings which enclosed it were short of paint and
rusty.

The house itself, built squarely of brick, needed pointing, the
woodwork looked as if the paint had been skinned off it, and the
outhouses, some made of old timber, were rotting. The iron grids
which once gave light to extensive cellars were choked with refuse
and almost corroded away.

When Littlejohn rang the doorbell, the familiar sign on the jamb
lit up dimly. *Enter.*

Through the dark, musty-smelling hall and past the ramshackle
old bamboo hatstand; and then the glass-panelled door to the
drawing-room.

'Come in.'

Scott-Harris was in his usual chair in front of the fire with his
feet on a stool. He looked feverish. His livid features appeared round
the wing of the armchair. He had been drinking heavily, although
it was barely past noon. He seemed relieved to see Littlejohn. He
didn't even greet him, but started issuing orders right away.

'Glad to see you. Just in time. That scoundrel Ryder's been out all morning and the coal scuttle's empty. Can't go and fill it meself. Blood pressure. Be a good fellah, and fill it. The shed's right opposite the back door. Straight ahead, through the kitchen, and there you are.'

Littlejohn seized the bucket and made off. The kitchen behind was large, old-fashioned and untidy. A sink full of unwashed dishes. Pots, pans, cardboard cartons, and empty food tins littered about. And over all, the stench of stale cooking and rotten fruit.

The flagged yard behind was dirty and neglected. Buckets, dustbins, ashes, and a trail of coal from a wooden shed to the back entrance of the house. Beyond, a wilderness of kitchen garden, untended, litter strewn about it, and overhung with the wrecks of old trees like those in the front garden. An old tennis lawn, too, with the grass all overgrown and decaying in a slimy mass. In the centre of the lawn, a smoke-blackened statue of a young goddess without head.

Littlejohn wrestled with the door of the coalshed, one of the hinges of which was broken, and filled the scuttle from a heap of coal dumped on the earth floor. A rat scuttered from a pile of old wooden boxes presumably there for firewood. The whole set-up was indescribably sordid and depressing. Littlejohn wondered what the rest of the rooms in the house were like.

Scott-Harris didn't thank him when he returned with his load.

'Put some on the fire before it goes out altogether.'

Littlejohn raked out the ash and filled the grate.

'The swine cleared away the breakfast dishes and I haven't seen him since. He's been behaving damned strangely of late.'

Littlejohn dusted his hands and sat down. He slowly filled and lighted his pipe.

'Before you settle, just go up to Ryder's room. Door facing you at the top of the stairs, overlooking the back. Can't make it meself. Heart's bad.'

First his blood pressure; now his heart. How long had he been sleeping on the couch if he couldn't climb the stairs? Littlejohn obeyed again. The old man evidently always behaved this way. Imposing on everybody who called during Ryder's absence. Still, it gave one a chance to look around the place.

The staircase was covered in shabby threadbare carpet, held in place by tarnished brass rods. The door of Ryder's room was closed. Inside, a plain iron bedstead, a cheap wardrobe, and a dressing-table, a sea of oilcloth with a mat at the bedside. The bed was unmade and the soiled bedclothes tumbled all over the place.

Littlejohn wondered what Ryder saw in such a job. Why he tolerated the old man and his Spartan lodgings. He must have been getting something good out of it somewhere. It wasn't like one of Ryder's type to put up with such conditions.

The Superintendent opened the wardrobe. Not a thing in it, but some old newspapers and a coat-hanger. The same with the drawers of the dressing-table. Everything swept clean. Not even an old safety razor blade or a piece of soap. A soiled towel hung from a hook behind the door. Littlejohn felt it; it was quite dry.

Littlejohn lit his pipe and stood with his hands on his hips, eyeing the room. No trace of its previous occupant, except some cigarette ends and spent matches in an old tin-lid used as an ash-tray, and a calendar hanging from a tack on the wall. He turned over the bedding. Unless he was mistaken, the bed hadn't been slept in. It had all the appearances of having been made and then deliberately tousled. Somehow, all the traces of a restless occupant were missing.

There was a battered straw waste-paper basket in one corner. Nothing in it. The fireplace had been boarded up and a small electric fire stood in front of it.

The window was closed and the room smelled stuffy and dusty. Between the two sashes was a wedge of paper, presumably to stop their rattling in the wind. Littlejohn took it out and unfolded it. It was a receipted bill, marked *Paid*, with the date of yesterday.

> *James Bidder*
> *Bespoke Tailor*
> *The Square. Basilden.*
> To One suit:... £25...

It must have been stuffed in the window last night. Queer, if Ryder was preparing to bolt, that he should be so particular about a quiet sleep, *and* about paying the bill.

'You've been a hell of a time!'

Scott-Harris was in the place and posture in which Littlejohn had left him. He looked like a huge, ugly balloon which had settled on a chair.

'I was just looking round the room, sir. Ryder seems to have packed everything and gone.'

Scott-Harris was so surprised that he sat up suddenly, only to subside again with a groan. He almost overturned the table on which the usual bottle, syphon, and glasses were standing.

'The hell he has! I bet he's been up to something. He's been behaving funny lately. Just like him to pack up and bolt at a time like this. Funeral tomorrow, and I've not had my lunch. Suppose I'll have to go out and get some food at one of the pubs. Damn the feller!'

He was thinking only of his own comfort, as usual.

'But surely, sir, you've missed him before this?'

'He gave me my breakfast. Then said he was off to do some shopping. He usually went out after he'd cleared away the dishes and didn't get back till around noon. He called at several pubs on his way back, guzzling with his pals.'

'Did he clean the house, too?'

'No. Mrs. Dommett, the char, comes every other day. Ryder could cook and saw to both our meals. Learned cookin' in the army and, by gad, he never improved. Still, with help so expensive and hard to get and my family not caring what happens to me, I was glad of what I could get. Now, what the hell I'm going to do, I don't know!'

'Had Ryder a police record?'

Scott-Harris's heightened colour turned deeper.

'What of it? No need to hang the dog for a bad name. I believed in givin' him a chance. Old soldier. He played fair. I kept an eye on him and he didn't misbehave.'

'How long have you had him?'

'About fourteen years. Came to me after he was demobbed in the last war. I knew him before the war. He was in my regiment.'

'What was he gaoled for?'

'Stealing army supplies.'

'That all?'

'And somethin' about car deals before the war. He's been straight since I had him. His last chance. But, damn it, don't stand there asking silly questions. You ought to be taking steps to find him.'

'Unless he's committed another crime, we have no authority to chase him. Leaving you without notice is a civil offence, not criminal.'

'Criminal? What the hell do you mean?'

'Unless he's stolen something. I don't suppose you've checked up.'

'How d'you think *I've* checked up? I didn't know till now that he'd bolted. Better get hold of Elvira. I can't handle this meself. Bad heart and blood pressure. I suppose Ryder got upset about Teasdale's murder. Always the same. Teasdale might have been born to annoy me. Ever since I first clapped me eyes on the fellah, he's gone out of his way to upset me.'

'I don't suppose Mrs. Teasdale's in a fit state to help you at present. The funeral and all that.'

'Well, one of the girls can come and do it. There's enough of 'em. Just get on the telephone... Ring the pub next door. The Royal Oak. Number's on the telephone pad.'

'I think you'd better do that yourself, sir. I've not called to fill Ryder's place, you know. I called to ask some questions.'

'What! More? You'll have to wait, then. I'm going to telephone myself, seeing you won't help me.'

He levered himself unsteadily out of his chair, flinging rugs and cushions about, and went with difficulty to the 'phone on a side table near the window. He was well able to do this for himself in spite of his semi-intoxicated condition, as Littlejohn knew. Scott-Harris raged at the landlord of the Royal Oak for making him wait until one of the Teasdale family was sought. Littlejohn had no idea which of them answered, but she received the full blast of the fat man's wrath and spite.

'... Ryder's bolted and I'm here on me own. One of you had better come up to see to things. He might have taken some cash or the silver. And I haven't had my lunch yet... I don't care if you are busy and upset. What about *me*? Your duty's to the livin', not the dead. There are four women in the house, surely one of you can spare the time for your helpless old grandfather...'

He hung up, swearing to himself, kicking cushions about. Finally, he camped in his chair and settled down.

'Pour me a drink and have one yourself. And be quick with your questions. One of my grand-daughters'll be here any minute and I want my meal. Trouble with you policemen is that you're always asking questions instead of gettin' on with the catching of criminals. What is it?'

Littlejohn poured him his drink.

'What about you?'

'I'm on duty, sir.'

'Don't make me laugh. Well? What else do you want to ask me?'

'Did James Teasdale call here with his wife about seven o'clock last Sunday?'

'He always brought her here in his old crock of a car on his way to his travels... Or should I say his hoop-la, now? Why?'

'Did he call in here with her?'

'Yes. Seemed to think he had to pay his respects. In one minute; out the next.'

The old man took a heavy swig of his whisky.

'That's better. I needed that.'

Littlejohn felt a wave of revulsion. He'd some horrible characters to deal with in the course of his duties, but this old man was the limit. Fat, gross, a glutton, alcoholic, there was an indescribable odour of evil and corruption about him.

'Exactly how long did Teasdale stay here?'

Scott-Harris waved his glass in the air.

'Five minutes, perhaps. He was never one who enjoyed my company, for some reason. Seemed afraid of me. Always uneasy when I was about. He knew what I thought of him.'

'Was there any conversation?'

Scott-Harris turned his poached, bloodshot eyes on Littlejohn.

'What are you gettin' at? You don't think I had anything to do with Teasdale's death, do you? I'm almost completely helpless, as you know. I couldn't walk the length of the street now, let alone make a trip to some godforsaken place near Ely, was it? Don't waste my time.'

'I asked you, sir, if Teasdale had anything to say when he arrived here last Sunday. You haven't answered my question. He quarrelled with his wife on the way. Was the quarrel continued here?'

Scott-Harris shed his rugs again and sat upright.

'Quarrelled? Who told you that?'

'It's enough that witnesses of repute heard them and reported it. Did you become involved in their quarrel when they arrived here?'

'I don't know what you're talking about. I know nothing of a row between them. Conjugal bickering... I won't have that sort of thing going on here. I don't want my peace disturbing. My daughters know that.'

'But did Teasdale know it?'

'He did. He merely called, as I said before, to say goodnight, and then he went off to his hoop-la and his other woman.'

'Did he mention his other woman last Sunday.'

Scott-Harris emerged from his cushions and struggled upright, livid with anger again, looking ready to attack Littlejohn.

'I told you, he said nothing. If you don't believe me, clear out. I've had enough of you. Coming here and...'

'Did he tell you he wanted his wife to divorce him?'

'Divorce? Who said anything about divorce? If he'd so much as mentioned it, I'd have chucked him out with my own hands.'

'I think you could, you know.'

'Don't get offensive. You've said enough. Instead of trying to find Teasdale's murderer, you're going around upsettin' everybody. Filthy insinuations. Dirty linen. I might have known. Well, I've had enough. Get out of here and stay out.'

Irene was arriving resentfully and purposefully at the rusty gate and walking up the shabby path, so Littlejohn took the old man at his word. He got out. Irene seemed surprised to see him. She perhaps thought he ought to have prepared the old man's lunch whilst he was there and generally deputised for Ryder, instead of calling out the mourners.

'Good day,' she said tartly, in greeting and farewell.

Bidder, the tailor, had a small shop in the square. The bell over the door tolled as Littlejohn entered. A weak-looking chair, shelves partly filled with rolls of cloth, old fashion-plates and cutting-books on a rickety table. Some of the dusty framed pictures of gentlemen dressed in what might have been Bidder's masterpieces dated back to 1900.

The tailor emerged from the room behind, which had a glass door inscribed *Fitting and Cutting Rooms*. There was a staccato clack of sewing machines somewhere in the rear.

Bidder himself was a small worried man with a pneumatic paunch. Elderly, with a shock of dishevelled grey hair, and knock-knees. He was in his shirtsleeves and wore gilt armbands to keep his soiled starched cuffs off his wrists. There was a tape-measure round his neck and chalk marks down his waistcoat, which bristled with pins like a porcupine, as well. He looked Littlejohn up and down from head to foot, pricing and appraising his tailoring. Then he rubbed his flabby hands.

'Well, sir. What can I do for you?'

His fingers twitched as though eager to seize and value the cloth of Littlejohn's lapels.

'Was Mr. Ryder a customer of yours, sir?'

Bidder's face fell so much that it entirely altered his appearance. No sale. He'd recognised Littlejohn from his picture in the local paper.

'Yes. I hope he recommended me to you. I'm very busy at present doing a rush job for tomorrow. The mourning suits for the late Mr. Teasdale's relatives. It was good of Mr. Ryder to send you to me.'

'I can't say that he did. He's left town. In his room, we found a bill from you which seems to have been settled this week.'

'That's right. I hope there's nothing wrong.'

'No, Mr. Bidder. How long did he owe you the twenty-five pounds?'

Mr. Bidder looked hurt. He began nervously to finger the rows of pins stuck in his waistcoat.

'Really, Superintendent! It's highly irregular to divulge customers' business. As you know, we tailors give long credit. We have to do so. Competition is very fierce and...'

'I see you know who I am, Mr. Bidder. Wouldn't it be wiser to assist the police in their enquiries?'

'If you put it that way, Mr. Littlejohn, I must agree with you. Especially as I'm a county councillor...'

What that had to do with it, Littlejohn never knew.

'... Let's say I'm relieved he paid up before he left town. Twenty-five pounds is a lot of money.'

'How long did he owe it?'

'Over eighteen months.'

'A long time, indeed. Were you pressing him?'

The tailor coughed politely behind his hand, as he did when fitting his best clients.

'I'm afraid I had to threaten him with a writ, sir. One must live. I cannot wait for ever for my money. I've my stock to keep up.'

'And when you threatened to sue him, Ryder paid up.'

'Yes. He called and paid in cash. I was very annoyed with him, I must admit. He'd always pretended how impecunious he was when I spoke to him about the debt. He even abused Mr. Scott-Harris for delaying in paying his wages. In my opinion, he was impecunious because of the amount he spent on drink and betting.'

'Why were you annoyed when he paid the bill finally? I'd have thought you'd be overjoyed.'

Mr. Bidder eyed Littlejohn reproachfully for being light-hearted about his troubles.

'I was annoyed to find out how much money Mr. Ryder really had. When he called, he produced the cash from a wallet absolutely bursting with money... even including a number of five-pound notes. And all the time he'd kept me waiting for my bill. It wasn't good enough.'

'Did he usually flaunt his money in that way.'

'Of course not. Had he done so, I would certainly not have waited so long before threatening to have the law on him. I have met him from time to time in local hotels where I call occasionally as a matter of necessary sociability, and there I've found him singularly hard up. He was known to cadge... if I may use the word... cadge as many drinks as his companions would pay for.'

'Thank you, Mr. Bidder. You've been very helpful. That will be all, thank you.'

Mr. Bidder coughed unctuously again.

'You will not, I hope, sir, divulge the information. A business like mine is based on discretion. It would never do for my clients to learn that I acquaint others with the amounts of their debts. I cater for a clientele composed of the best people in the district and I must be careful of my reputation.'

He sounded like a banker, anxious about his overdrafts.

'Of course, Mr. Bidder. Good day.'

Littlejohn tolled himself out.

It was raining again and the streets were muddy and miserable. Most of the population were at lunch and the square was deserted. A man who sold washers and refrigerators on H.P. was leaning against his doorpost looking miserable. He glared at the clouds overhead and wondered when the credit-squeeze was going to break and the sun come shining through again. A funeral passed; a hearse and three cars. The occupants of the last taxi were laughing among themselves. They seemed to be enjoying it.

Mr. Evans of the Swan with Two Necks was standing in the vestibule watching the passers-by. He spotted Littlejohn and made a pantomime of letting him know that lunch was ready. He tapped the bill of fare framed in a brass case to the left of the door, and rubbed his stomach to indicate that it embraced something appetising. Littlejohn signalled that he wouldn't be long.

He called at police headquarters and asked them to send out a general enquiry, particularly to police stations in an area roughly bounded by Bradford, Selby, Birmingham and Ely, for any news of the Black Arley Sedan, VB3007, Teasdale's car found near the Dumb River last Monday. He needed information gathered between 7.0 p.m., and 7.0 a.m. on last Sunday night.

He also asked them to institute enquiries about Ryder's movements since his disappearance.

Then, he went to his belated lunch.

POSTE RESTANTE

CROMWELL HAD TELEPHONED FROM SHEFFIELD. HE'D BE IN Basilden before nine. Littlejohn had dined, but had still an hour to spare before meeting his colleague at the station. Now, he was pushing open the door of the Bull's Head, a new hotel built on the housing estate on the fringe of the town.

All around, the council houses spread as far as the eye could see, most of them lit up. Some hadn't drawn the curtains and through the windows you could see families gathered round the table, busy at their evening diversions. In one house a small boy was practising the cornet; in another three girls were seated, heads down, doing their homework. Rows of electric street lamps illuminated the scene and, in a railway siding, they were noisily shunting trucks.

There were half a dozen of them round the bar, working men, well washed, in their going-out clothes and cloth caps, drinking beer. Another quartet were playing darts, as though the fate of the world depended on their throws. Their glasses stood on a marble table.

'What'll it be, sir?'

The landlord himself attended to Littlejohn. He was a little emaciated man, unlike the traditional publican, with a face like a greyhound's and a small waxed moustache.

'A bottled beer in a tankard, please.'

'There's a snug across the lobby. You'll find it a bit quieter there.'

'I'm quite happy here, landlord.'

'Suit yourself.'

The room was hot and lighted by a single large electric lamp in a frosted globe. Advertisements for beer, cigarettes, and potato crisps hanging on the walls; beer pumps, and a few buns on a stand protected by a glass cover; a middle-aged barmaid, heavily made up, blonde and with a huge bosom, washing glasses and operating the beer-pumps. Rows of bottles on shelves behind, and a broken watch hanging over a sign. *No Tick. Please do not Ask for Credit, as a Refusal often Offends.* The place was foggy with tobacco smoke.

The landlord was at Littlejohn's elbow, showing him the label on the bottle he was holding.

'It's the best that money can buy. A real good line.'

'Did Chris Ryder ever call here?'

The landlord smiled a knowing smile and then winked at Littlejohn.

'I hear he's done a bunk. Bit of a slimy sort. A drink cadger, too. I never took to him. Yes; he used to come here one or two nights a week. He did the rounds of most of the pubs in town. Sort of levied a toll of drinks as he went from one to another, slapping his pals on the back and waiting for them to stand him one. Wonder where he's bolted to.'

He prised open the cap of the bottle and carefully poured the beer in a tarnished pewter tankard.

'Was Harry Wood one of his friends?'

'Yes. Why?'

'I'm just wanting a word with Harry. I called at his home address and his wife said I'd find him here.'

'That's him.'

A middle-sized, full-chested, swarthy chap of middle age. He had a shock of black curly hair and thick lips. He was waiting for his turn at the dartboard. It was obvious from his patronising manner, that he thought himself a cut above the rest and was merely playing with them as a favour. He flung his first dart. He wasn't much good at the game.

'Harry. This gentleman wants a word with you.'

The landlord turned to Littlejohn again.

'Haven't I seen you somewhere before?'

An elderly man with a grizzled head and large even false teeth turned from the counter. He'd been seeking an opening.

'You've seen his photo in the *Gazette*, Leonard. It's the detective from London. Am I right?'

It was his turn to wink now. He looked from one to another of his companions, proud of himself.

'That's right.'

'And what does Scotland Yard want with me? Going to arrest me?'

Harry Wood stood in front of Littlejohn. His eyes shone with drink. Another shifty sort, a second-rate singer with a Chaliapin repertoire to which he'd never in the world be able to do justice.

'I wanted to talk with you about Ryder. I believe you knew him.'

'Chris? Yes, I knew him right enough. Any idea where he's hiding himself? I heard in town this afternoon that he's vanished.'

For one who sang Figaro's songs as encores, Harry Wood was singularly ill-spoken, humourless, and loud-mouthed. He seemed as if he couldn't do anything without an audience.

'Let's have a drink at the spare table in the corner, Mr. Wood.'

'Don't mind if I do.'

He looked all round to see that everybody was noticing his importance.

'Same again, landlord, please.'

Harry Wood winked at the rest to show he was master of the situation and that Scotland Yard wasn't going to put anything over on him.

Any more of their winking and Littlejohn felt he'd probably start doing it himself. With some of them it was like a nervous tic.

They sat at another marble top, which the landlord mopped free of beer with a damp cloth.

Harry Wood thrust his face close to Littlejohn's. He smelled heavily of beer. That was what had prevented his reaching the top flight of bass singers. Beer. Beer and swank. He was swanking now. He felt he was in the public eye and was determined to hold the stage. He emptied his glass in one.

'Same again, Leonard. Come on, Superintendent. You're slow.'

The landlord served them.

'These are on the house.'

'You knew Ryder?'

'I said so. Through meeting him here, that's all. He fancied himself a bit of a musician. He'd once played the cymbals in a regimental band.'

He said it loud enough for all to hear. His eyes roved round the room, like a second-rate opera singer's.

'*I* can't tell you where Ryder is.'

'I don't suppose he'd be likely to tell you. I came to ask if, at any time, you told him that you'd met James Teasdale with his hoop-la stall at Lowestoft Fair.'

Wood frowned. He was a bit taken aback by the sudden question.

'Who said I'd seen Teasdale and who told you I mentioned it to Ryder?'

All eyes were on Littlejohn this time. It was awkward trying to get information from this conceited half-drunken singer in front of an audience, but it didn't matter much. Littlejohn didn't lower his voice.

'You were in Norwich and he was in Lowestoft, not far away, at the same time, weren't you? Teasdale with his hoop-la at the fair; you singing at the musical festival.'

Wood recovered at the mention of singing.

'I reckon they didn't treat me fair there. I admit I was off colour. I'd a hell of a cold. But I reckon I put on one of my best shows for all that. I never sang "Chronos the Charioteer" better. Know it? It was the test piece.'

'You took a day off in Lowestoft and you saw Teasdale?'

Harry was in the limelight again. An important witness. He was going to make the most of the job. The man with the teeth and grizzled hair interrupted him, however.

'You never told us, Harry.'

'Why should I tell you? I'm discreet, if I'm nothing else. He's dead now, so it doesn't matter. But while he was alive, I didn't want to do him a bad turn by blowing the gaff and letting his wife know. You see, he'd a woman with him. A smasher, too. A young bit of stuff like a gipsy. A perfect Carmen and I wouldn't mind singing with her in opera either. Where is she now that Jimmie Teasdale's gone? I wonder what she could see in him.'

'So you told Ryder all about it?'

Wood's face darkened. He eyed Littlejohn defiantly.

'So what?'

'He was as likely as anybody to tell the family, wasn't he?'

'Of course he wasn't. I just thought he'd be tickled to death to hear about Jimmie being a Don Juan. Imagine Jimmie singing Don Juan's serenade...'

Wood thereupon bellowed a few deep lugubrious bars and looked round for admiration. None came. They were all watching Littlejohn.

The man with the false teeth couldn't contain himself.

'That was a good one. Imagine what old Scott-Harris would have said if he'd got to know his precious son-in-law was running a bit of young stuff at the fair...'

'Shut up! Who's asking you?'

'Look here, Harry...'

The landlord intervened.

'That'll do, Tom. The Super wants to question Harry. You don't often get a chance to see a thing like this, you know.'

It was developing into a rickety-rackety Irish comic scene. Littlejohn and Harry Wood fighting it out at the bar like a lawyer and a difficult witness and the rest like the public in court, half drunk, their mouths open with curiosity.

'What you want to know for?'

'I want your help, Mr. Wood. It seems nobody knew of Teasdale's double life till you told Ryder.'

'Who told you? Did Ryder?'

'No.'

'Who did, then?'

A fresh trio of customers appeared in the doorway and stood like pillars of salt, trying to make out what was going on. The landlord put his finger to his lips dramatically to keep them quiet and winked at them, too. They tiptoed in and shut the door with exaggerated gestures. One of them was drunk already.

'Who told you?'

'We have our own sources of information.'

'Somebody was listening in, then, while I was talking to him quietly. It was in here. At that table in the corner. Somebody with long ears.'

He glared at the man with the teeth.

'You've no need to look at me. It wasn't me. I've something better to do than listen to other people's gossip.'

'What did Ryder say when you told him?'

'I told him to keep it dark. It didn't seem fair to spoil Teasdale's bit of fun. He's had a lot to put up with from his wife. However, he must have blabbed it all over the shop.'

'He didn't.'

'Then somebody overheard what I said.'

The others had lost heart. They had been expecting something dramatic, some revelation which would take Harry Wood down a peg, but now the Superintendent was drinking up and getting ready to leave.

'Did you speak to Teasdale at the fair?'

'I said how-do to him, if that's what you mean. He was surprised to see me, I can tell you. He turned pale at the sight of me. And then he pretended he didn't know me and said I must have mistaken him for somebody else. As if I had. Why, I'd know him anywhere, in spite of his dark glasses and his fancy suit.'

'You don't mean to say he was disguised? Well! That beats the band.'

Nobody took any notice of the man with the teeth. They were now hanging on every word again.

'And that was all. You left him without insisting?'

'I left him. I wasn't going to have an argument or a row with him, although I could willingly have punched him on the jaw at the time for the high-handed way he talked. Mistaken him for somebody else, indeed! It *was* Teasdale. And you could have knocked me down with a feather when the girl suddenly appeared and asked him for small change. You could tell by the way they behaved, too, they were sweet on one another. I'll bet they were carrying on. If his wife had got to know, she'd have killed him. But I wasn't going to be the one to spoil his bit o' fun.'

'Somebody did.'

Dead silence. A man with a squint, munching potato crisps with toothless gums at the end of the bar, stopped chewing.

'Tell us some more about the girl,' he said.

They all laughed with relief. Harry Wood put his thumbs in the armholes of his waistcoat, thrust out his chest, and looked pleased with himself.

'That's one thing I won't do. I found her first.'

The landlord and the barmaid started refilling the glasses.

'Have this one on me, Super.'

They were all anxious to buy Littlejohn a drink. Scenes like this didn't happen every night. They'd have a lot to talk about afterwards.

'I must be going. I've to meet somebody.'

'The murderer?'

It was obvious they'd find things a bit flat after Littlejohn left, but he bade them all goodnight and made for the station.

Outside it was raining again. The curtains of all the windows on the housing estate had now been drawn and the place seemed asleep. Littlejohn had to pick his way among the puddles of rainwater which lay about the uneven pavements and in the road. Beyond the estate it was worse. Here, private builders had been having a field day. A short stretch of unadopted road was riddled with potholes half-full of soft clay and water like cold tea. In the dark loomed the silhouettes of half-built bungalows, excavation machinery, and concrete mixers. There wasn't a soul about.

When he arrived at the station, the ticket collector told Littlejohn that Cromwell's train would be late. Someone had put a sleeper across the line a mile away and the diesel had run into it.

'It's a mercy it wasn't derailed. We've sent a steam loco to pull it in to Basilden. It won't be long.'

Eventually Cromwell arrived safe and sound. There didn't seem much wrong with the front of the diesel, but Control, whoever that might be, had insisted on precautions. The driver of the steam locomotive was jeering at the man in the diesel cab.

'You want to get a proper engine...'

Littlejohn was glad to see Cromwell again. He was fed up with ploughing a lonely furrow in the back o' beyond. Cromwell was lugging the bag which he always had with him when they were on an important case together. It held everything necessary from law books to handcuffs and finger-print tackle. He was wearing his cap, too, which implied either that he was taking his ease or there was a wind about somewhere. They found a stray taxi, drove down to the Swan with Two Necks, installed Cromwell in his room, evaded Heck, and ordered supper for an hour later. Then they went to the police station where Littlejohn introduced his colleague to the personnel, which consisted of a sergeant, a constable, and the reporter of the local paper, who was busy writing up the cases dealt with in the day's petty sessions. The rest of the usual staff had gone to the policemen's ball, which was going on in the town hall two doors away. They could hear the drums and saxophones churning out a foxtrot and a large car was leaving with His Worship the Mayor, wearing his chain of office and a top hat.

The sergeant in charge could hardly wait for Littlejohn.

'Inspector Naizbitt told me to send for him to the town hall if you called. He's got some news for you.'

'I don't want to disturb him if he's dancing at the ball...'

'But them was orders. He said I wasn't to forget 'em. Here, Banks...'

The constable ran to the desk and saluted briskly. This quite took the sergeant by surprise, as he wasn't used to it. Banks was putting on an act for the benefit of Littlejohn and Cromwell.

'Banks, go and fetch the Inspector...'

Banks ran out like a good boy.

'... The Inspector 'll be glad to come. He 'ates dancin', but has to attend as a matter of jewty. Proceeds in aid of police charities, you see. Now the Mayor's left, they'll start rockin' and rollin' and whatnot. Inspector Naizbitt's missus is a bit younger than him and she likes a rock an' roll now an' then. Then, she puts 'im through the 'oop, good and proper. Makes it difficult for discipline, sir...'

Naizbitt was on the doormat, beaming with pleasure. He was wearing a dinner suit and his black tie was half-way round his neck. He looked to have run all the way. In the town hall the band was starting to play 'Knocking and Rocking My Baby'. The saxophones were screaming and through the uncurtained windows you could see couples throwing one another about.

Naizbitt straightened his tie and smoothed down his hair.

'Come in here, sir.'

The sergeant blew into his moustache. It wasn't good enough telling Littlejohn the news in secret.

The Inspector's room was cold and it took him a long time to light the gas-fire which kept exploding and emitting yellow flames instead of blue. Eventually Littlejohn was able to introduce Cromwell, who was now wearing his bowler with great dignity. Naizbitt said he was pleased to meet him and Cromwell said the same in return. Then Naizbitt found them a chair apiece and sat down at his own desk, a weather-beaten relic of better times, and rubbed his hands.

'I've some news for you, sir.'

The sergeant entered with cups of tea. Naizbitt seemed surprised. He didn't usually bring in the tea himself, but sent it in by a subordinate. Now the sergeant hoped to linger and hear the great news. Instead, he was thwarted. Two constables brought a roaring drunk in the charge-room and the sergeant had to return to deal with him. He was shouting the place down.

'They're all drunk at the police ball. Why can't I get drunk, as well? One law for the rich and another for...'

Dead silence. Littlejohn wondered what they'd done to him.

Naizbitt was full of news.

'We've had some replies about the all-stations call for information about Teasdale's car, sir.'

Between Chatteris and Benwick, in the Isle of Ely, the police had reported seeing the car, 'number as stated, description as per enquiry.' There had been a flood diversion on the road over which the river had overflowed. A patrolling constable had stopped the car, turned him round, and told him the best way.

'It was driven by somebody different from Teasdale. Description didn't tally at all. The driver did his best to keep his face hidden. He wore a black slouch hat, didn't speak a word, and avoided the light. The report said they couldn't give any description.'

'Not much help. What time would that be, Naizbitt?'

'Four-fifteen a.m.'

'The time could be right.'

'But the other report is much better. Grantham say that at 2.0 a.m. the policeman at Long Bennington stopped the same car without a rear light. Faulty connection. It came on again when the driver shook it. The constable had reported it, but said as it was pouring with rain and the driver said he was anxious to get to Cambridge and had been delayed by the floods up north, he exercised his discretion and let him proceed with a caution. I wish he hadn't, although he'd probably have got a false name and address. In spite of his efforts to avoid being seen, the constable got a good look at the driver once or twice. Do you know who I think the description sounds like...? Not Teasdale, by any means...'

'Ryder?'

Naizbitt's face fell. He looked thoroughly disappointed.

'You knew all the time?'

'I guessed. It couldn't have been Teasdale. He was dead before he got to Long Bennington. He must have been in the car, folded up in the boot, probably dead before he left this town. He hadn't digested his supper, you see. If he'd been alive at Long Bennington, his supper would have long been past his stomach.'

Naizbitt scratched his head.

'I'm not well up in anatomy, sir.'

'Well, that's a bit of good work, Naizbitt. Thank you for the help.'

'That's not all. Nobody's seen or heard of Ryder. He seems to have vanished from the face of the earth. But there's one thing that's queer. His letters.'

Outside the street was full of music and the sounds of stamping feet. The Mayor's departure seemed to have let loose an avalanche at the town hall.

'What about them?'

'The deputy postmaster called here this afternoon. He'd heard we were making enquiries for Ryder. Every morning, almost as soon as the post office opens at eight, Ryder calls for his letters, which are kept poste restante. Perhaps he has correspondence he doesn't want old Scott-Harris to know about, or perhaps the old man's tampered with his letters in the past. Be that as it may, Ryder won't have his mail delivered to the house. He calls for it. Yesterday and this morning he did something he's never done before. He didn't call at all. His mail's still there. I couldn't take it away. We've no authority for that, but I had a look at it. Four or five envelopes; two sealed, betting letters by the look of them. Three unsealed; a paid bill, and two lots of pools coupons.'

'So you think that if Ryder were leaving for good, or even temporarily, he'd have called for his mail before he went and as likely as not, arranged for it to be re-addressed.'

'Yes, sir. Don't you agree?'

'Yes, I do. What do you think, Cromwell?'

'The same as both of you. Do you think there might have been foul play?'

'That's one inference. We've got to find out. There's one thing, however. If Ryder thought we were on his trail about the death of

Teasdale, he'd bolt without mail or anything else. To go for his post might have run him right in our hands.'

'Why would Ryder want to murder Teasdale?'

'He might have been blackmailing him. Harry Wood met Teasdale on his hoop-la stall with his woman at Lowestoft and told Ryder when he got home. Ryder might have been squeezing Teasdale.'

Cromwell rubbed his chin.

'But Teasdale *wanted* to get a separation or a divorce from his wife. He told Martha Gomm and she had to make him promise not to do anything rash for the present.'

'Perhaps Teasdale was trying to keep his promise when Ryder started the blackmail.'

'But, if Ryder murdered him, he'd be killing the goose that laid the golden eggs.'

'Perhaps Teasdale attacked him and got killed in a fight. Martha Gomm said he was a little terror when his temper rose. She told me that he attacked her own husband, twice his size, in a rage, and laid him out.'

'If we admit that, why should Ryder take the body all the way to the Dumb River to dump it?'

'In Teasdale's pocket diary was written the place where he was due to be on the following day. To leave the body in Basilden would have narrowed the search for the murderer considerably. Ryder thought he was being clever. He took the body and left it with the car where it was expected to be. Anybody might have murdered Teasdale there. His enemies on the fairground, some of the riff-raff who follow fairs, even Martha Gomm. It would have been a very complicated case and might never have been solved. Ryder thought it all out but forgot one thing, and a very likely thing to be forgotten, too. He forgot the undigested supper in Teasdale's stomach. That, in effect, brought the body all the way back to Basilden.'

'Where do we go now?'

'Cromwell and I are going to the Swan for a cold supper. Care to join us, Naizbitt?'

From the town hall, the noise was louder than ever. Things were warming up. Now, they were 'Watching All the Girls Go By'.

'It would have to be in the way of duty, sir.'

'We can arrange for that, Naizbitt.'

When Heck Evans entered his dining-room later, he recoiled in surprise to see Inspector Naizbitt in full dinner rig, eating cold Melton Mowbray pie and pickles and drinking Hock with his two colleagues.

Heck himself had just slipped across from the police ball to see that everything at the Swan was orderly and in good shape. He and his wife were running the bar at the dance. He was in full evening dress, tails and all, but he'd put on a black tie to make himself look like a real maître d'hotel. Instead, as his coat was a size too large, he looked like a hired hand.

THE FUNERAL

I T WAS FINE, BUT THE STREETS WERE COLD AND DAMP. THE church clock was striking ten as Littlejohn and Cromwell entered the police car which was taking them to the cemetery for James Teasdale's funeral. The atmosphere of the town was not funereal at all. It was market day and stalls had been erected in the space in front of the town hall. There an exuberant crowd of stallholders were already shouting their wares, mainly eatables, with here and there a dash of clothing or cheap jewellery. The place was seething with life. Dominating all that was going on and looking slightly disapproving of it, was the stern bronze statue of Bishop Duddle, the only famous man who ever was born in Basilden. He had been martyred and eaten by cannibals of his diocese in the South Seas and now stood among the market folk, pointing to heaven, indicating the place to which he had gone after all his troubles.

As Littlejohn and Cromwell joined the police car, a hearse passed through the square and pulled up at the door of Teasdale's shop. Although it was yet empty, many of the market men removed their caps in tribute, knowing whom it was going to serve for the last time. The corporation garbage-cart, which was busy emptying the dustbins on one side and which stood in a row on the edge of the kerb of the square, because the backs were inaccessible to vehicles, halted out of respect, and the dustmen lined up beside it, bareheaded, to watch the event.

If his wife's family hadn't thought much about James Teasdale, other people evidently had. In happier days, it seemed, James had been an infant prodigy in the town band. He'd played the euphonium in the never-to-be-forgotten year when the band had won a third prize at the Crystal Palace Festival. There were still some survivors of that triumph, eight of them, and they had gathered in front of the shop with their trumpets, drum, and uniforms. They got busy forming fours ahead of the hearse. They were going to play James to the cemetery. And, for a period during the war, Teasdale had been an auxiliary member of the Basilden fire brigade. Four uniformed firemen added themselves to the band. Also, although the dead man had not attended their lodge of late, James had been a freemason. Two carloads of his brethren arrived and parked round a corner, looking ready to ambush the main party when it appeared.

If the widow had hoped for a quiet funeral, she was going to have a surprise!

The undertakers' men arrived like a quartette of hired assassins and entered the shop. The coffin and floral tributes were carried out. A crowd surged round, murmuring sympathetically. The owner of a stall selling poultry, sausages and cheese wiped his hands on his apron and ran to join the rest, and a dog which had been hanging round thereupon stole a cock chicken and ran off holding it by the neck.

The mourners emerged, all in black. Mrs. Teasdale looked bewildered at the crowd and then hesitated, appalled at the sight of the band, now forming up with instruments at the ready.

'Who are those men?'

Barbara had been forewarned and had consented to the music, but had forgotten to tell the family. Now, fearful of a scene, she hustled her mother in the first cab. The rest followed, surprise at the band and firemen driving all looks of despair and resignation from their faces. The procession moved off, slowed down by the speed of the band, which struck up the *Dead March in Saul*, which they played all the way to the cemetery gates; then they changed to Chopin's *Funeral March* along the tree-lined avenue to the graveside.

James Teasdale was going to be buried in the grave of his family. It was as though, having heard of the newly discovered irregularities of his life, his wife had insisted on returning him to his own people, and, in due course, resting herself in peace as far away from him as possible. The headstone had been removed from the grave and lay on one side as though flung away. *Reginald Teasdale, died 1934, aged 66 years. Maude Elizabeth Teasdale, his wife, died 1942, aged 68 years.* And the names of three of their children who had died young. *R.I.P.*

Major Scott-Harris was not among the mourners, who included all the rest of Teasdale's own and his wife's families. Cousins from a distance, a very deaf old man whom nobody seemed to know, and then a mob of townspeople, curious because they'd never been at the funeral of a murdered man before.

Littlejohn and Cromwell stood on the edge of the crowd. It was the Superintendent's habit to attend such events; you never knew what you might see and hear.

For the most part, the dead man received public sympathy. A decent, hard-working chap, with not an enemy anywhere. People were surprised that anybody should want to kill Jim. Some of them eyed Littlejohn with satisfaction, as though sure he would bring the criminal to justice and let the victim rest in peace.

Scott-Harris came in for a lot of criticism. He ought to have been there. If anybody excused him on the strength of his being an invalid, there was invariably the retort that he could get around when it suited him.

The daughters gathered round Mrs. Teasdale, all dressed in the deepest mourning. It was evident they were having some trouble with her. She wasn't in tears but looked to be in a state of collapse. As the coffin was lowered, she fainted and they had to carry her to the nearby chapel to revive. It caused a stir of sympathy. Littlejohn didn't miss the look of fear, almost terror in her face just before she passed out. It was as though she expected the dead to rise and rebuke her.

The minister, the vicar of the parish church, resumed the committal timidly... It was then that Littlejohn caught the eye of a woman in black on the edge of the crowd.

It was Martha Gomm. She hesitated as he looked at her, wondering whether or not to recognise him. Finally, she buried her face in her handkerchief. He did not see her again. She vanished in the crowd, which was breaking up. She had come a long way and was returning as far, simply to be there at the end. Before he left, Bertram, examining the funeral tributes, discovered that a sheaf of red carnations had insinuated itself among the rest. *To James, with love.*

'Where did that come from?' he asked his wife, who was with him.

They looked blankly at each other and Bertram was uneasy. He didn't like it at all and cautiously picked it out.

'That must have come from some other funeral,' he said to a gravedigger. 'Remove it.'

The gravedigger, hurrying anxiously to collect the price of a drink from the undertaker, could think of no better place to fling the flowers than in the open grave. So Martha Gomm's red carnations lay on top of the coffin when the last earth fell upon it.

They had revived Mrs. Teasdale and the mourning party boarded their carriages and drove off. The band, left in the air, looked a bit lost and then, joining the firemen, went off to the pub at the gates, the Cemetery Hotel, for a drink. The crowd began to melt away; some to catch buses back to town, a short distance; others to examine the wreaths or inspect nearby graves. Littlejohn and Cromwell made for the police car again.

'Excuse me.'

A man in grey, with a tired solemn face, stood at Littlejohn's elbow.

'Excuse me. Are you the Scotland Yard detective?'

'Yes, sir. What can I do for you?'

'There's something I think you ought to know.'

He didn't seem the sort you asked to come for a drink and a talk.

'Would you care to come with us to the police station, sir? We could talk in comfort there.'

'It isn't much. I can tell you here. I must get back to my work. I've only asked off for a couple of hours. I felt I had to see the funeral. He was always a good friend of ours. Even in his hard times, he gave us what he could.'

'You represent some charity, sir?'

'The Salvation Army. We have our Citadel a few doors away from Mr. Scott-Harris's house.'

Littlejohn knew the type well. Serious, decent, truthful.

Another funeral was approaching.

'Let's sit in the car, then, sir, and you can tell me what you wish.'

The man climbed in and sat on the back seat.

'It may not be significant, but it's said in the town that James Teasdale was not killed where they found him. It was reported in one of the daily papers. It said it seemed that he'd been murdered in Basilden and the body carried to where they discovered it. I don't want to waste your time, but I think...'

He licked his lips and seemed diffident. He was shy of wasting the time of the police on what might be a triviality.

'Last Sunday we held our usual evening service and it was my turn on duty. You see, whilst the service is on, one of us stands at the door to encourage interested passers-by to come in and join us. We start at half-past six and end about half-past seven. After the general service, there's a devotional gathering at eight and casual visitors often stay on to that. I was at the door for over an hour, starting about six-fifteen to seven-thirty. It was rather cold and wet and I sheltered in the vestibule, but regularly went to look up and down the street... just in case, you see.'

'I understand.'

He did, too. He'd once attended such a service himself when a criminal had sought refuge there and he'd sat and waited until it was over.

'I wanted you to know that on that night there were some strange coming and goings at the Scott-Harris house, which is almost opposite the Citadel.'

'Just tell me exactly what happened, then, and my colleague will take it down in his notebook.'

Littlejohn offered him his cigarette case, but the man shook his head.

'Thank you. I don't smoke. Well, first of all, just after seven, the Teasdales arrived there in their car. I'd recognise it anywhere. They called at that time every Sunday as a matter of habit. I've often seen them when it's been my turn on duty. He brought his wife to see her father, saw her indoors and then, as a rule, he'd leave about ten minutes later, presumably to go to wherever he was travelling for the week. He was a commercial traveller, you know.'

Obviously the whole scandal – the fairground saga and Martha Gomm – wasn't yet public property. Harry Wood had probably told the truth. He'd kept it dark for his own purposes.

'... This night, however, he stayed indoors longer. Whilst he was inside, there was another visitor. I knew him, too. A man called Harry Wood. He's a singer and has been singing at the Citadel sometimes. That was about ten minutes after the Teasdales arrived.'

Through the car window, Littlejohn could see the second funeral
ending. Not so elaborate, this time. Probably third-class. There was
a mere handful of mourners, who seemed a happy lot. They were
parting from one another in a frenzy of handshakes, like a party
dancing the lancers.

'Twenty minutes later, about seven-thirty, Wood came out and
hurried away. I went inside after that, but my friend, Grimes, who
followed me on duty at the door, told me later that about 8.30, Mr.
Scott-Harris's servant... I've forgotten his name...'

'Ryder.'

'That's it. Ryder. He drove Teasdale's car, which was standing
in front of the house, round the street at the side of the house.
It's just a sort of cul-de-sac which leads to the old coach-house. I
know that part, because when the Salvation Army first came to
Basilden years ago, Mr. Scott-Harris rented the stables to them.
They cleaned them out and used them as a citadel for some time,
until Mr. Scott-Harris said they made too much noise and told
them to leave. They hadn't much money in those days and the
rent was low...'

'And that's all you have to tell me, sir. Thank you. It's been most
useful...'

'I haven't finished yet. Excuse me if I'm taking up a lot of your
time. It's probably no use at all. You'd find it out yourself, I'm sure.
But I thought...'

'Please go on, Mr...'

'The name's Smith. John Smith.'

'And your address, sir?'

Mr. Smith suddenly seemed to realise that Cromwell was there
and was surprised.

'Fifteen, Duddle Street. Shall I go on?'

'By all means, sir.'

'At about nine-thirty, as we were finally leaving the Citadel, I saw Teasdale's car appear from the back and Teasdale drove away.'

'Did you actually see Teasdale?'

'Not really. It was pitch dark outside, except that there's a lamp in front of Scott-Harris's front gate and a patch of light made by our windows and doorway just opposite the Citadel.'

'So, if the car was driven, from the back, one couldn't see who was in it.'

'No. It's a saloon and there are no lights inside. In fact, I think what made me remember it was the fact that there was something wrong with the rear light. It kept bobbing out and then in again.'

That was right! It had conked out altogether later in the night.

'And that's all, sir?'

'I'm afraid it is. I don't suppose it's of much use, but seeing the matter is one of murder, I had it on my conscience a bit.'

'It's most useful, sir. And now we'll take you to town.'

It was noon when they arrived back. The market was still going it full steam and was now crowded by work people taking their lunch-time break. The dog was there again, seeking another chance to snatch a chicken. The owner of the stall, unaware of its former treachery, was feeding it with pieces of cheese-rind, which it chewed with disdain.

At the police station there was still no news of Ryder. Trains, taxis, buses had all been subjected to enquiries, but nobody had seen the batman.

'What does Harry Wood do for a living apart from singing bass?'

Inspector Naizbitt looked bewildered.

'How does he come in it?'

'He saw Teasdale at Lowestoft Fair and told Ryder about it. He was also seen entering and leaving the Scott-Harris house last Sunday night whilst Teasdale was there.'

Naizbitt whistled.

'Was he, now? He always seemed a decent law-abiding citizen to me. However, one never knows. He's a cashier in a local tannery. We'd better pull him in if you want to question him. You'll not find it pleasant meeting him at the works. The stench is terrific.'

'Will you send for him, then? We'll have some lunch at the Swan and be back here at two-thirty. Scott-Harris wasn't at the funeral.'

'It's not to be wondered at. He couldn't stand Teasdale. All the same, you'd have thought, being it's one of the family, however much he hated him, he'd have put in an appearance. I suppose he thought it infra dig some way. Shall I send round and find out what's happening at Rangoon?'

'I think not. We'd better go ourselves after we've seen Harry Wood. By the way, what state of health is Scott-Harris in?'

'Not bad. For one so heavy, he seems to get about quite well. A bit short of breath and florid; but what can you expect? I guess he'll drop dead one day, however, in some awkward spot and give us a lot of trouble. I hear he was out of doors at half-past eleven.'

'Whatever was he doing? If he could come to town, surely he was fit enough for the funeral.'

'You might guess. The licensed wine-shops were just open and he was in town buying whisky. With Ryder missing, he's having to do his own chores. He must have run out of whisky drinking to Teasdale's safe departure.'

'He drove to the shops, I presume?'

'Yes. That's how we knew. Parked on the wrong side, as usual, and gave a lot of back-chat to the constable who told him about it. He didn't get booked, however. Some of his old pals are still on the bench and it's a bit awkward dragging him in front of them. He drove off quickly with half a dozen bottles, so our man didn't persist. He said that Scott-Harris seemed much the worse for wear. He was either ill or tight. He could hardly hold himself together.'

At the *Swan*, Littlejohn and Cromwell lunched in a small room at the back. The usual dining-room was fully occupied by Teasdale's mourners. Mrs. Teasdale had been excused on account of her recent collapse, and the rest were enjoying a good meal. Drinks, too, judging from the noise, and, as the two detectives passed the door, they saw one of the elderly relatives making up for his recent compulsive sadness by slapping a buxom waitress on the behind.

13

THE WITNESS

HARRY WOOD WAS IN HIS WORKING CLOTHES WHEN LITTLEJOHN found him at the police station. He didn't look at his best. He wasn't in a good temper, either.

'I wish you'd confine your enquiries to times when I'm not supposed to be at work. What does it look like, a bobby turning up and saying I'm wanted at the police station? To say nothing of asking off and having to explain what it's all about. Couldn't it have waited?'

'You wouldn't have been bothered at all, Mr. Wood, if you'd been a little more forthcoming last time we were together. Where were you last Sunday night?'

Wood's little dark eyes grew even more shifty than usual. Littlejohn couldn't help associating him with opera and now he thought how well he would look as the hunchback in *Pagliacci*, first singing the prologue, and then hatching out a double murder.

'That's easy...'

Harry Wood's self-confidence returned and he smiled affably.

'I was singing at the British Legion concert. Anybody'll tell you that, if you want an alibi.'

'Where did you call on your way to the Legion?'

'Look here; this is a bit thick. I hope you don't suspect me of... What is it you're after...? The murderer of Jim Teasdale? I was in Basilden all night on Sunday and half the town can prove it.'

'Where were you between seven and seven-thirty?'

'At home, getting ready to keep my engagement at the Legion.'

'You were not. You were at the Scott-Harris home until seven-thirty. What were you doing there?'

'I don't know what you're talking about. Whoever told you that is a liar.'

'I'll have to tell you, then, Mr. Wood. Some time ago, you saw and recognised James Teasdale in Lowestoft. You admitted that.'

'I did. I was honest with you and this is what I get. You're trying to mix me up with this murder.'

'You told Ryder, who, in turn, told Major Scott-Harris. The old man could never resist a chance of taking Teasdale down, of humiliating him. Here was just what he wanted. A big row with Teasdale. He'd been ashamed of his son-in-law ever since he married his daughter and he was eager to get a cheap revenge on him. He wasn't content with denouncing him on the mere information given by Ryder. He had to go the whole hog and face Teasdale with the man who'd seen him at Lowestoft, with his hoop-la stall and his other woman. He arranged with Ryder for you to be there when Teasdale and his wife made their usual Sunday evening call.'

Harry Wood looked round the room as though seeking someone to witness the rubbish Littlejohn was talking. Instead, he met the cold eyes of Cromwell and Inspector Naizbitt.

'Where did you get that tale? Has Scott-Harris told you?'

'If you wish to be faced by those who saw you, I can arrange it. But it will be the worse for you. I believe that during or after that meeting, James Teasdale met his death. If you don't want to be mixed up in a murder case, Mr. Wood, you'd better co-operate quickly.'

Wood licked his lips. He hadn't had a shave for the day and he was beginning to sweat with fear. He looked a bit like a thug, now.

'I was only there for a few minutes. I was asked by Ryder to call and confirm the story he'd told Mr. Scott-Harris. The major half thought Ryder had made it up. He thought that if I turned up unexpectedly it would give Jimmie Teasdale the surprise of his life. And, by gad, it did!'

'Tell us exactly what happened.'

Wood looked more at his ease now. He fished in his pocket and took out a soiled packet of cigarettes.

'No smoking in here,' said Naizbitt.

'You've a nerve! Here I am helping the police and...'

'Get on with it, man.'

'I think I'd better. The sooner I get away from this oppressive atmosphere, the better I'll feel. As you said, Super., Ryder asked me to call. Teasdale and his missus were there.'

'What were they doing?'

'Mrs. T., was sitting in a chair by the fire. Jimmie was standing up as if they hadn't asked him to take a seat. There'd evidently been some high words, because when I got inside, Jimmie was looking very annoyed and red about the gills. Mrs. T. was snivelling. The major never even said good evening to me. All he said was, "And here's the man who saw you. It's no use denying it." From which I gathered the whole thing was out and they were having a row about it.'

'And then?'

'Well, I was a bit puzzled. It didn't appear to me that Teasdale was even trying to deny it. He didn't seem surprised when he saw me. Old Scott-Harris's little plot had fallen flat. The only thing my calling there brought out was that Jimmie must have been trying to find out how Scott-Harris got to know about his double life, and when I turned up, he knew, you see, because of our meeting in Lowestoft.'

'So, you left right away.'

'The old man gave me a drink...'

'And the rest...'

'What do you mean?'

'You aren't trying to tell me, Mr. Wood, that you took all that trouble just for a drink. Let's say, as you would when you're out singing, that you got your fee.'

'You suggesting that I was doing a bit of blackmail?'

'Exactly… Ryder was a snivelling little wretch. It's my opinion that he could hardly wait to see James Teasdale on his next return to Basilden. He thought Teasdale would probably pay anything to keep his double life dark. Instead, he found the opposite. Teasdale didn't care. He told Ryder to make the whole thing public. That was just what he wanted. He actually wanted his wife to divorce him. Ryder, the little sadist, hatched a neat revenge on James when he was shown the door. He told Scott-Harris and added that if he didn't believe him, he'd bring the man who'd actually seen Teasdale leading his other life and face him with you in front of his wife. Scott-Harris evidently jumped at the idea. And that's why you were called in.'

'Well? That's what I've told you. Nothing wrong with that, is there?'

Littlejohn didn't seem to hear what Wood was saying.

'If you were in any way involved in blackmail, Mr. Wood, you will tell me right away. I intend to get to the bottom of the whole affair, every detail of it. I won't let go until I do. If you, later, appear in the case again as a blackmailer, I assure you that you'll be charged with that offence, which won't mean a fine, but gaol. Now; what have you to say?'

Wood was sweating again. Drops of perspiration ran down the sides of his face and lost themselves in the stubble of his dark beard.

'I tell you, I didn't have anything to do with blackmail. I can't say any more than that. Teasdale's dead and Ryder's vanished. You've only my word. If you won't believe me, you can ruddy well charge me with blackmail.'

But he'd have wanted anything but that, judging from the looks of him. In the words of Naizbitt later, Wood was scared stiff.

'Did Ryder tell you he'd blackmail Teasdale?'

Relief for Harry Wood. The subject was moving from himself to someone else.

'Come to think of it, he suggested that Teasdale would be anxious to keep it quiet.'

'What was that if not blackmail?'

'I didn't see it that way at the time.'

'When you left Scott-Harris's house, what was happening?'

'As far as confronting Teasdale with me went, the whole shooting-match had fallen flat. I stood there looking silly while Teasdale gave old Scott-Harris and Ryder the length of his tongue. I always thought Jimmie was a mild sort of chap, scared to death of the old man. But not this time. He started to tear strips off old Scott-Harris.'

'What do you mean by that?'

'He called him a damned old bully. Them's the words he used. He told him he'd had enough of him and his nonsense and he wasn't standing for any more of it. The old chap nearly had a fit. Then Teasdale turned to his wife and said he was sorry; and he looked it. It seemed to distress him to have to tell her the truth. But I didn't hear any more. Old Scott Harris turned on *me*. "What are you hanging about for? This is a private and family matter. You've caused enough trouble. Clear out." Something like that. I was so surprised that I hadn't a word to say. I just went. But I like his damned cheek, after I'd taken the trouble, at his request, to call and confirm what I'd seen.'

'Didn't Teasdale say anything to you at all?'

'He was just going to, I think, when Scott-Harris opened the door and told me to go. He was starting to say to me… "And as for you…" I wish he'd said it. If he'd insulted me, too, I'd have knocked his block off. I didn't want to have a row with the old man. He's nearly twice my age and might have had a stroke if I'd turned on him. But Jimmie Teasdale… I wouldn't have stood any lip from him.'

'Was he going to say something about blackmail to you?'

'I've told you, I never had a thought of blackmail. It was Ryder.'

'Well, I'm glad we know that. And that'll be all for the present, Mr. Wood. We'll probably meet again.'

'I hope not. I've had enough.'

He put on his cap and made off as fast as his legs would carry him. As he passed through the square, people turned to wonder what all the hurry was about.

Littlejohn lit his pipe and strolled round the room idly, seeing nothing, lost in thought. Then he glanced through the window which overlooked the square.

The workpeople had returned to their factories and offices and the market was almost deserted now. All the bargains had gone. The man with the cheese and chickens had sold up and was packing up his belongings and dismantling his stall. Fruit salesmen were altering their prices, chalked up on brown paper bags and stuck among the fruit on the end of a stick. Oranges at 4d. each in the morning were now four for a shilling. A man who sold curtains was holding an auction sale. He was drunk already and now and then gave away a length of material for nothing.

The funeral party was leaving the Swan and breaking up until another member of the family, near or distant, turned up his toes. There was a lot of handshaking and half-hearted kissing and most of the relatives scattered in all directions, some to the 'bus depot; others to the railway station. Two old men were going off in a taxi. In the end, only the close relations of the dead man remained, uncertain what to do next. Sam Geddes, the corn-chandler, and his wife looked out of place and disdainful. They were both almost teetotal and had resented the goings-on in the main pub of the town. Cornford, the registrar, and Chloe, the olde-tyme dancers, were with them, and Teasdale's brother, Bertram from the Water

Board, who seemed more at a loose end than anybody else. Bertram's wife, a sufferer from migraine, had had one of her headaches at the graveside and had gone home to a darkened room and vinegar-and-water compresses.

There was some argument or other going on. It was obvious what it was about. The Geddes pair were anxious to call at the shop and give Elvira some more comfort. Bertram was trying to persuade Walter Cornford to join him for a drink at the club. He looked parched and restless. It was plain to see where the club was located from the behaviour of Bertram's glowing nose. He looked like a pointer, rigidly fixed in the direction of his quarry. Finally, they settled it. Bertram and Walter went off to the club, three doors from the town hall; Chloe almost tearful, joined the Cornfords and they all strolled uncertainly in the direction of the Teasdale shop, as though wondering whether or not they'd be welcome there after all.

Littlejohn knocked out his pipe in the old-fashioned grate.

'I think I'll go and have a drink with Bertram and Walter. I won't be long. Meanwhile, old chap, you and Naizbitt might see to getting a search warrant for the Scott-Harris house. We've got to face it and give the place a thorough look-over. I've tried to avoid it. The old man's been a J.P. and there might be some resistance. However do your best.'

Naizbitt looked dumbfounded.

'You surely don't think the old man…?'

'I don't know.'

'Teasdale, or Ryder?'

'I'm interested in Ryder. He may never even have left the premises. There was some jiggery-pokery going on there the night Teasdale died. There's no other way of finding what it was all about.'

Bertram and Walter were surprised to see Littlejohn, who'd had to show his warrant card to the caretaker to get across the threshold of the club. An old house converted in better days. Once it must have been sumptuous, judging from the woodwork and shabby ornamental ceilings. Now it was seedy, almost on its last legs. The kind of place a town like Basilden couldn't support any longer. Bad oil-paintings and stiff photographs of members of the political group who'd founded the place, hanging on the walls. Antiquated fittings, threadbare carpets, cold old-fashioned chairs upholstered in chilly leather.

The two men were sitting before the smoky fire of the reading-room. There was nothing to read there, but it said so on the opaque glass door. They had glasses of double whisky each and a syphon between them on a marble-topped table which looked bow-legged with age.

'Hullo, Super. Thinking of joining the club? There are plenty of vacancies. When I joined thirty years ago, there was a long waiting list.'

Bertram was jolly by way of reaction after his enforced solemnity. The drink felt to do him good. His nose glowed. Both he and Walter were heavily in mourning. Black suits, black ties, all-black socks. Walter had hung up his black bowler with his black gloves balanced on the rim. Bertram was, as usual, wearing his hat.

Littlejohn went straight to the point.

'I came to see if either of you knew much about Chris Ryder.'

'He's missing, isn't he?'

It was too banal an answer and Walter realised it. He went to the door and shouted up the stairs for Joe, the caretaker.

'Whisky for the Superintendent... Make it a double, Joe.'

There was no bar and Joe simply produced a bottle and a glass from a cupboard and gave Littlejohn careful measure. Then he raised an eyebrow at Walter and Bertram and filled up their glasses, too.

'Ten an' six...'

Walter left Bertram to pay whilst he splashed soda in the glasses.

'Good health to you. You were saying Ryder…?'

'Yes. Did either of you know him well?'

Bertram pointed his glass at Walter.

'*He* might. I never had much to do with him. Or with Scott-Harris for that matter. I resented the way he treated my brother, who was as good as he was any day.'

When he mentioned his brother, Bertram briefly raised his hat. Walter laid an affable hand on Bertram's arm.

'Don't take on so, Bert. James is past it all now. He's at rest.'

They must have had one or two before Littlejohn joined them. They were a bit maudlin now.

'Ryder. As Bert says, I knew him. Never fancied him, either. He had too much influence over the old gentleman.'

'Where was he born?'

'Here. In Basilden. Knocked about the world a bit when he grew up and the major met him somewhere on manoeuvres in the Territorials. Both coming from Basilden gave them a bond in common and the major seemed to take to him.'

'Has Ryder any relatives here?'

'Not now. He'd a sister, but she married and went off to Canada, I think. That's right, Bert?'

'That's right, Walter. Canada.'

'Oh, you needn't think, Super., that Ryder's run off to join her across the Atlantic. They weren't on speaking terms for years. Ryder did a stretch in gaol for something or other. Can't remember what it was. His sister disowned him after that. She was a religious sort of girl. I can't think what the major could see in him. We were all surprised when he turned up and said he'd taken him on as his manservant. But you know what Major Scott-Harris is like. He must have his own way.'

'You're tellin' me,' said Bertram and belched loudly.

'Pardon me.'

'I gather Ryder backed horses and was always broke.'

'That's right. You get around a bit, don't you, Super? Who told you that? Ryder even tried to borrow from me now and then.'

The door opened and another man in a bowler hat thrust in his head. He had a mournful bloodhound's face and large hands with which he clung to the door, hesitating whether or not to come in. Finally, he made up his mind.

'Afternoon, Bert. Afternoon, Walter. And good afternoon to you, sir. I can see you want to be left alone. I suppose you're talking over matters with the lawyer. I'll leave you to your business. Good afternoon, all.'

Bertram looked flabbergasted.

'Who the hell's that?'

'I don't know.'

'He knows us.'

'I've never seen him in my life before...'

Littlejohn was fed up with it all. The two men seemed to have nothing to do but idle the time away in their potty little town and let the rest of the world go by.

'Just before he vanished, Ryder seemed flush with money. Where did he get it?'

'When was that?'

'Monday, I believe.'

'That was the night Bidder mentioned it in the club here. Remember, Bert?'

'Yes. Something about paying his bill from the wad of notes...'

They were starting again!

'How did he come by it? Can either of you guess?'

'Perhaps the old man owed him his wages for a month or so, and paid up. I know the major kept him waiting sometimes until he drew his quarterly cheque under his wife's trust. Last Monday, Major Scott-Harris 'phoned my missus and asked her to lend him fifty pounds. He'd had some expenses in the house, he told her, and had gone through his last allowance completely. The next cheque wouldn't be in for six weeks.'

Bertram looked at him owlishly.

'And did she cough up, Walter?'

'Yes. She called the same night with the money. She's always been a good daughter to him. The old boy was off colour. After he'd taken the cash, he fell asleep. I wonder if he owed it to Ryder and paid him with it. If he did, it was a bit thick.'

'As you say, Walter, it was a bit thick.'

'Can either of you gentlemen make a guess as to what's happened to Ryder? Had he any friends, that you know of, that he might have gone to visit? Or did he ever absent himself for long from his duties?'

Walter emptied his glass.

'Not that I'd know. Have you asked the major?'

'Yes. He's no idea where Ryder's gone. His room was emptied of all his belongings and he seems to have quit for good.'

'In that case, he might be anywhere. A wonder he didn't pinch the old man's car while he was at it. He was a very light-fingered one, was Ryder. The major's cigars and whisky were never safe when he was about. He even picked the locks of the tantalus and the cigar drawer...'

There was nothing more to stay for. The two men were evidently settled for the afternoon and would end in helping one another home.

'Thank you very much, gentlemen. I'll get back to duty.'

'So long, Super. Good luck.'

It was three o'clock. Another funeral was passing through the square. The fire engine was turning out, too, in full blast. Everybody seemed to stop work and emerge from shops and offices, watching the firemen's progress. There was never a dull moment in Basilden, even if it was a one-eyed town.

'Cassons' stocking works is on fire,' someone shouted.

Then the Geddes pair appeared in the square, boarded a waiting bus, and vanished. They must have left Walter Cornford's wife at her sister's and, judging from their sulky faces, there'd been a row of some kind.

At the police station, the sergeant-in-charge greeted Littlejohn apologetically.

'I'm sorry, sir, but they've not got the search warrant, yet. It's a bad day. Market day, when most of the magistrates are out of town. They called at Colonel Hough's, but he said there wasn't a good enough case and he wouldn't give the warrant. If you ask me, it's because him and Major Scott-Harris was in the Territorials together. Dr. Royle, another magistrate, is out on a confinement and wont be back till, at least, four o'clock. So, they went to try Mr. John Casson, who's always a help. But, they look like being unlucky there, too. The fire engine's just gone out to a fire at his works. If they ask him for a search warrant at a time like this, he's likely to turn the hoses on them. He's a man with a temper. They'll find somebody else, sir, don't you worry.'

'I'm sure they will. Meanwhile, I think I'll take a stroll to Mrs. Teasdale's and see how she's getting along after her bad bout at the funeral. If Sergeant Cromwell returns, tell him to join me there and we'll go together with the warrant and see Major Scott-Harris.'

He made his way along the usual route to Teasdale's shop. The door was still locked and the blinds were down. He rang the private bell and Chloe Cornford answered.

'Good afternoon, Inspector… I mean, Superintendent. Did you want to see my sister. Come in…'

She stopped him in the dark shop to whisper a word or two in confidence.

'My brother-in-law is annoyed because I gave Elvira some brandy. She was so upset by the funeral. She fainted, you know. I got a small quantity from the public house next door and gave her a spoonful and it did her a lot of good. But my sister, Phoebe, and her husband are temperance workers, and we had words about it. They left in a huff. I'm just explaining that if you get the smell of brandy when you speak to my sister, it's only been taken in the way of medicine and it's all my fault.'

Littlejohn could hardly keep his face straight. If Chloe could see her husband's condition in the club just now, he thought, she'd have a lot more apologising to do.

Chloe led him in the now familiar living quarters behind the shop.

'Here's the Superintendent calling to ask how you are, Elvira.'

The widow looked completely relaxed. More even than usual. Chloe must have given her a pretty stiff dose of medicine! She didn't know whether to laugh or cry when Littlejohn entered.

'It's good of you to call and enquire, Superintendent. If it wasn't for Chloe, I'd be all alone in my grief. Chloe was always my favourite sister. I don't know what I'd do without her. The girls have gone to the station, all three of them, to see Aunt Julia and Uncle Toby off on the train. Aunt Julia and Uncle Toby are very wealthy members of my family. The girls have great expectations from them…'

She wouldn't stop talking. If Littlejohn hoped to get any useful information from her, he'd have to change his tactics. Being a good listener wasn't going to lead anywhere.

'Do sit down… I'm sorry I didn't get up to greet you. I'm not well. My legs will hardly hold me up.'

She was slumped in the rocking-chair, moving to and fro, as usual.

Chloe went to the hearth and poked up the fire. Then she went and filled the kettle and set it on the hob.

'I'll make some tea.'

'I hope you feel better, Mrs. Teasdale.'

'Yes, thank you. Chloe gave me some brandy and would you believe it, although it was only medicine, Phoebe and Sam were annoyed about it and said it was disgusting. I told them that if that was the way they felt about it at a time like this, they had better go home before they upset me more. So they went.'

'Your father was too upset and ill to attend the burial, I hear.'

She hadn't once looked at Littlejohn and she spoke again without facing him.

'That's right.'

Just that, as though she wanted to drop the subject.

Littlejohn sat in an armchair beside the table, which was littered, as usual, with teacups and plates with crumbs and pieces of cake on them.

Mrs. Teasdale had kicked off her shoes and kept rubbing her feet along the carpet as she rocked, as though they pained her.

Littlejohn found it hard to think of anything to say. He'd hoped to ask about last Sunday night, but felt it was hardly the time. Mrs. Teasdale might dissolve into hysterics.

'I'm upset. It always makes me ill. I've been through such a lot this past week. Today at the cemetery, I suddenly came over with the feeling I always get when I cut myself and see blood. I went all hot, then cold, and then I knew nothing more.'

'I'm sorry the past week has been so hard for you. When did it all begin? Last Sunday night, after your husband left you?'

She looked up this time, fear in her eyes.

'You always ask me questions when you call. It isn't fair. I've nothing to hide. Although they told me that he wasn't a commercial traveller at all, but earned his money at a disgraceful job on a fairground, I wouldn't have wished him dead. Even when I heard he had another woman, I still wouldn't have wanted him killed. They oughtn't to have done that to him.'

'Would you like to tell me about it all? It will do you good to get it off your mind.'

'Tell you about what?'

Chloe was back with some clean cups. She paused, listening to the conversation.

'Tell him, dear,' she said a length. 'He'll help you. None of us others can. You're afraid to tell the children and you say you daren't confide in Sam and Phoebe. You'll help her, won't you, Superintendent?'

'I'll do all I can for you, Mrs. Teasdale, but I must first know what it is all about.'

Mrs. Teasdale suddenly began to cry. Huddled in her chair, she whimpered like a child.

'Don't rush me, both of you. I've got to have time to think. With all I've been through, my head aches and I can't think. I never thought he meant it, you see. Even when they told me James had been murdered, I still thought someone had done it where they found his body. Then, when they said he was killed in Basilden and his dead body taken to that other place, it dawned on me. He *had* killed him. He said he would kill him, and he did.'

'Who had killed him?'

They could hardly hear her answer for her gurgling and sobbing.

'Father.'

14

FRACAS ON SUNDAY NIGHT

C HLOE RUSHED TO HER SISTER AND TOOK HER IN HER ARMS.
'Don't say any more, dear. You're not well.'

And then she turned on Littlejohn. Good temper had left her face and her eyes flashed with anger.

'Can't you see she's ill. She's overwrought with the funeral and all she's been through. Shame on you to question and bother her at a time like this and in her present state.'

But Elvira wanted to talk. She said so in a voice muffled by Chloe's motherly bosom to which her face was being forcibly pressed. Elvira had found relief in a single accusing word. Now she wanted to tell everything.

Littlejohn sat quietly, his hands relaxed on the arms of the old wooden chair. It was a fight against time. If the train came in promptly and removed their rich relations, the daughters would soon be home. And that would terminate their mother's confidences.

'Let her go on if she wishes to, Mrs. Cornford. It's all bound to come out sooner or later. We will discover the truth. Even now, we're searching for Ryder. He will know everything and tell it, perhaps to the disadvantage of your father. Let your sister give me a plain statement and I'll do all I can to make things easier for all of you.'

Chloe stood silently holding her sister; then she relaxed.

'Do you want that, Elvira?'

'Yes, I do. I think Mr. Littlejohn has been the most sympathetic of all of you. He took us to Ely to bring James home and he isn't the sort who would do an unkind trick. I think he knows all about that happened, but I want to tell him myself, too. Let me do that, Chloe. I'm sure he'll be kind to Father. He's an old man and Mr. Littlejohn will see he's treated mercifully. If anybody else finds out, Father will have a bad time.'

Littlejohn was seeing another Mrs. Teasdale. One whose every hope and happiness had been shattered by family pride. Now, she had no more pride left and humanity was beginning to show through the broken case-hardening of a lifetime.

'When they put James in his grave, it came to me how hard he'd tried and how little I'd helped him. I even left him with the house-work to do because he couldn't afford a maidservant. And when the girls were babies, I blamed their being born on him, and made a nursemaid of him, too. He went wrong and disgraced himself to get money for me and the family, and if he took up with another woman, perhaps it was because he never got anything but complaints and spite from me. He's dead now and it's all over. I ought to tell Mr. Littlejohn how it happened. I owe it to James. It's the only thing I can do if I ever want to sleep again.'

All in a dull monotone, almost a pleading tone of voice, as though seeking someone to take her confession and forgive her for the thoughts which haunted her.

Chloe stood dumbfounded.

'I don't know you, Elvira. Whatever's made you like this? I...'

'When father didn't come to the funeral, as he'd promised, I knew *he* did it, and was afraid. I hated him then. I think I've always hated him. It was through him, wasn't it, bullying and discouraging us, that we ruined our married life? He turned the girls against their own father and made them despise him by always picking on him. I hate him now for all he's done to me.'

Chloe didn't say a thing, but stood there, tight-mouthed, amazed at the flow of words coming from her sister. But she didn't try to stop them. Perhaps she, too, felt the same about Scott-Harris. Littlejohn thought of Walter Cornford, whom he'd left at the club, drunk in the middle of the afternoon, aware of the old man's contempt for him, too.

Scott-Harris had lost his only son, the apple of his eye, and took it out of the men his daughters had chosen.

'Give me another dose of brandy, Chloe. Then I'll tell the Superintendent everything.'

Chloe gave her a keen look. Then she went to the sideboard, rummaged inside it, produced the bottle, and poured out a table-spoonful. Elvira lapped it up.

'Don't put the bottle away. I may need another dose.'

It might have been the first steps in sin, the way Elvira carried on!

Chloe put the bottle on the table to avoid further argument, but kept a wary eye on it. Almost a quarter of the brandy had gone.

Littlejohn guessed why Elvira was so tearful and talkative, so different in outlook, almost sentimental. She had had more than one dose of brandy. Chloe, the soft-hearted member of the family, had been giving Elvira tablespoonfuls of courage and comfort! Well, it was better than drugs.

'I thought James seemed different, somehow, when he came home last week-end. He was more independent and manly; and much happier about something. I thought his business must have been doing better.'

Perhaps that was what she had wished for all along. A more virile and courageous husband who'd stand up to her bullying father, instead of the timid little nobody she couldn't respect. As for the change in Teasdale's outlook and manner… She hadn't heard about Martha Gomm's expected baby. Perhaps now, she never would.

'I thought James had been up to something or other, but he never said a word until we got to Father's, last Sunday night.'

It was a bit rambling and Elvira kept looking from one to the other of the two listeners, seeking approval.

'On the way there, we called for some petrol. I was quarrelling with James at the time. He talked of coming home once a fortnight, or even once a month, instead of weekly. That's when I first started to suspect him. He'd been travelling for years and never once missed returning every week-end. I spoke to Father about it in front of James.'

Littlejohn could imagine it. Elvira denouncing James to her father, and the old man's caustic reaction. He couldn't bear Teasdale and any excuse for reviling him was always welcome.

'What did your father say to that?'

Elvira gulped and looked eagerly at the brandy bottle, but Chloe didn't take the hint.

'He said he'd expected it. And then he said right out that James wasn't a commercial traveller at all, but ran a low-class game on fairgrounds and was living with another woman when he was away from home.'

She began to cry again. Her face contorted frightfully and the tears flowed unchecked down her cheeks and ran off the tip of her chin.

Chloe clasped her sister to her again.

'That's enough for now, dear. If you must talk about it all, wait till another time when you feel better.'

Elvira stopped her weeping as though someone had turned off the tap of her tears. She pushed her sister angrily away.

'I won't stop and I won't wait till another time. I've started this and I'm going to finish it. I shan't sleep till I do. I haven't slept a wink since Monday.'

Littlejohn remembered that she hadn't lost her appetite, however, and he doubted whether she'd spent many sleepless nights either. However, no use arguing...

'Father said that, at first, he hadn't believed it himself. It was Ryder who'd told him about it, and Ryder often embroidered the truth. But Ryder had produced the man who'd actually seen James and his hoop-la and his other woman at Lincoln Fair...'

'Lowestoft.'

'I said you knew all about it, Superintendent. What did I say, Chloe? He knows. I knew it was a cathedral city somewhere in the east. Well, Father said, so that I could have it from the horse's mouth, he'd asked the man who'd seen James to call while I was there. "I've done it," he said, "because I know you'll try to make me a liar if I don't prove it to you. So I'm going to face you both with him for the sake of the family and to prove what a little rotter you're married to."'

Littlejohn could see old Scott-Harris gloating over it.

'James got in a terrible rage. He hadn't expected it. He usually just dropped me off at Father's and went on his travelling. But this time Father had insisted on him coming in, as he'd something he wanted to see him about. Have you a cigarette on you?'

Chloe's eyes almost shot out.

'But you don't smoke, Elvira!'

'I do. When nobody's in, I smoke Irene's. She has some in the end drawer. Pass the packet. I don't care now who knows that I smoke.'

Littlejohn handed her his case and lit her cigarette. She puffed at it like an old hand.

'The man arrived before James had time to say very much. An awful man. I knew him by sight. His name was Jasper Wood...'

'Harry.'

'It doesn't matter. Jasper or Harry, it makes no difference to his awfulness. I've heard him sing in the *Messiah* at the local Methodist chapel. His voice is in keeping with his looks. He just said he'd seen James at Lincoln with his stall and that woman, and he turned and asked James didn't he remember. He looked very pleased with himself and sneered, because he said James had snubbed him at Lincoln. And James actually lost his temper again and slapped Jasper Wood in the face, and Ryder who was present and Father had to go between them and stop a fight. I've never seen James so furious. Ryder, in the end, took Wood to the door and told him he'd better go, which he did.'

She was talking now as though relating incidents which hadn't cut deeply into her own life. She'd forgotten her part in the drama and sounded almost casual and objective. Littlejohn began to wonder if recent events had upset her mental balance.

'After he'd gone, James suddenly turned on Father, and I've never heard the likes of what he said to him. I'm sure Father's never had such a telling-off in his life before. He called him a bully, a self-opinionated nonentity, an impostor and a hypocrite. He even used bad language. I'd never heard James swear before. He must have learned it from the fairground and the woman he'd been associating with.'

Then, she lowered her voice dramatically.

'He finally said he wanted a divorce from me, as he couldn't bear the life he was leading any longer. Father didn't ask him why. He told him he'd see that I never divorced him, and I agreed with Father. To think of him going off with a fairground trollop... Well, at the time, I felt I'd been insulted, and so did Father. "I'll kill you for this, Teasdale," Father shouted. "So you'd better look out." And he went and pulled down a sword from the wall and drew it, and began to wave it about. Ryder took it from him. So Father opened the door and told him to take himself off to his woman and his hoop-la, or he'd throw him out himself.'

Chloe sat down breathless in the nearest chair. She couldn't believe it! Brawling in the Scott-Harris family!

'And James went, Elvira?'

'No, he didn't. He ignored Father. He even laughed at the sword and the threats. Father might just not have been there. He turned on Ryder, who'd been hanging about all the time, saying nothing, but taking it all in. He said to Ryder, "So you've carried out your threat and told the major, have you?" It seemed that Ryder had been trying to get money from James to keep quiet. He'd even sent James a letter about it. James had refused to pay and Ryder had done what he said he would, blown the gaff, as James vulgarly called it. James said he was going straight to the police about it, as they had ways of dealing with blackmailers. He said he'd enough evidence for them. Ryder laughed, denied he'd ever done such a thing, and said James was simply venting his spite on him.'

'And did your husband leave after that?'

'He was just going and made for the door, but Father called him back. He said he wanted a word in private with him, as it looked as if James was going to start a family scandal and he wouldn't stand for that. He said he wanted it settled then and there. And he told me to go and wait in the morning-room, as I'd been upset enough already. I said I'd rather stay and hear it out. Father got mad again and roared at me to get out and do as I was told. I saw there'd only be another fight if I didn't. So I went. I was too upset even to argue.'

And once more, she began to weep, but went on talking through her sobs.

'I must have been in the morning-room a quarter of an hour – no more – and I could hear them shouting in the dining-room. At one time they sounded to be running round and round, but before I could go to see what it was all about, there was silence again. After about five minutes, I went back. James had gone and Father was there alone.'

'What time was it?'

'About nine.'

'And you got there about seven. Was all this going on for two hours?'

'Yes. I haven't told you all the details, but the quarrelling went on for so long, and the men would reach the end of one quarrel and then start again about something else. I think they must have gone through all the family history since James married me, and some previous to our marriage. Now and then, they'd stand glaring at one another for what seemed an age, and then James would make for the door and Father would call him back and they'd begin all over again. It was a nightmare. And there was I, standing, struck dumb, having to listen to it all. I might just not have been there. James usually left about seven, but he seemed to have made up his mind to have it out once and for all, this time.'

'And you stayed on after your husband had gone?'

'Yes. I went home about half-past ten.'

'What made you say your father had murdered your husband?'

'He said he would, and if Ryder hadn't prevented him when he took down the sword, I'm sure he'd have injured him then.'

'You think he killed him whilst you were in the morning-room?'

'When else? Father was flushed and upset when I returned. He could hardly speak and when he did, his talk was all mixed up. I thought he was going to have a stroke. I got him some brandy and stayed with him a bit. Then he said he'd be all right; I'd better go. I asked him what had happened while I was out of the room. He said he'd tried to talk some sense into James and that James had gone to think it over. He'd be back at the week-end.'

'Where was Ryder whilst all this was going on?'

'He must have retired to his room or else gone out. I usually stayed to supper on Sundays, but none was laid. I asked Father if I'd better get us some, but he said he wasn't hungry and would just have a drink and go to bed when I'd gone. Later, when I heard what had happened to James, I was sure they'd had another quarrel after I'd gone in the other room, and that Father had taken the sword again and killed James. You remember the wound was a stab in the back. The noise I heard was Father chasing round the room after James. He must have caught him and killed him. That was why Father was so upset when I found him.'

It sounded fantastic. A real bit of old-time melodrama, concocted by some unsophisticated eccentric. Furious father, chasing round the betrayer of his daughter with a sabre and cutting him down to avenge the family honour!

'What do you think happened to the body? How did it come to be discovered in the Dumb River, near Ely?'

'I think Father or Ryder must have hid it till I left and then taken it there. To make it look as if that woman had done it. I wish she had. It doesn't seem right to accuse my own father of doing it. But it was my husband who was murdered, however unfaithful he'd been to me, and I won't sleep again till the truth has been found. I can't see how else the body got to Lincoln.'

'Ely.'

'It's the same.'

There was a silence.

'What are you going to do?'

'I'd better call and see Major Scott-Harris. I'll ask him what he has to say about it all.'

'Don't tell him what I've told you, will you? It might not have been Father, after all. It might have been somebody else.'

'Who, for example?'

'It might have been anybody. A robber, or a hold-up on the way after he'd left Basilden.'

'But how would such a person have known to take it to the Dumb River? I'll have to make enquiries...'

The bell on the doorpost was ringing and Chloe hurried to let in the visitors. Littlejohn bade Mrs. Teasdale a hasty good-bye and followed Chloe out.

It was the girls returning from seeing off their rich relatives. Two of them had their boyfriends with them, which might have explained the long time in returning from the station. Littlejohn was hastily introduced to the doctor and the bookie as he left, but didn't retain much impression of them. He was too dazed by Elvira's dramatic recital. He thought the doctor looked like a bookie and the bookie like a doctor, and wondered if they'd got mixed up in the confusion of introduction. The last he heard was the girls saying the train was very late arriving to carry away their aunt and uncle, and Elvira's voice asking Chloe if it wasn't medicine time again.

15

FAMILY DIFFERENCES

AT FIVE O'CLOCK IN THE AFTERNOON, BASILDEN WAS LIKE A dead town. The factories had not yet finished for the day, the women were off the streets preparing their evening meals, the shops were empty. Nobody much about, except the knot of gossiping old men who, as long as daylight lasted, seemed to hang around the corner of the square, talking interminably. All their eyes were on Littlejohn as he made his way back to the police station.

There was nobody in the police station except the sergeant-in-charge and a solitary constable attending to the telephone and sorting out files.

'Inspector Naizbitt and Sergeant Cromwell not back yet?'

'No, sir. They must be having difficulty in finding a magistrate. Several of the J.P.s are at work or out of town, and Mr. John and Mr. Jabez Casson, who usually do emergency work, are probably too busy with the fire at their factory to attend to their public duties. The fire's still burning. All our spare men are out there and we've had to close the main street that leads up to the station. It looks as if one side of the factory might collapse and fall across the road. They've had to send for the brigades from Haystonbury and Lindale to help...'

As if to confirm it, a large fire engine clanged its way through the town and vanished in the direction of the fire.

'I think I'll make an informal call on Major Scott-Harris then. When they arrive with the search warrant, you might ask them to join me at Rangoon and then we can get on with the job.'

Two policemen thereupon entered carrying a man who looked as though he'd been celebrating the fire. At that early hour, he was dead drunk. The two bobbies did their best not to be rough with him as they struggled to the cells, but he made it difficult. He writhed to free himself, cursed them profoundly, and said what he would do to them if they'd give him a chance.

Littlejohn walked to the Scott-Harris home. All the police vehicles were out but it only took ten minutes to get there on foot.

The house looked more gloomy than ever. Not a sign of anyone at home. The light was on at *Enter* and Littlejohn pushed open the door and found himself in the dark hall. Nobody bade him enter the living-room where Scott-Harris always made his headquarters, so he knocked and went in.

Major Scott-Harris was lying on the couch in front of the fire, which had almost burned out. He looked ill this time. All the ruddy colour had vanished from his cheeks, leaving a network of purple veins behind. He was breathing heavily. The usual whisky and soda and the plated tray were at hand.

'How-de-do, Littlejohn. Thought you'd be calling again. You don't seem able to keep away. What is it this time?'

'I suppose I'd better make up the fire again, sir.'

'I'd regard it as a favour if you would. One or another of Elvira's brood ought to have been here by now. Expect they've taken the huff because I didn't attend the damn' funeral. I didn't feel up to it. Hate the blasted cemetery to start with, and I hate more a crowd of weeping relations all tryin' to look upset and wondering at the same time what sort of a meal they're goin' to get when it's all over. Did you go?'

'Yes, sir.'

'Why?'

'It's part of the case and I thought it my duty to be there.'

'Can't see any duty in it. I guess you were keepin' an eye on the principal characters of the tragedy. Did it go off all right? No scenes?'

'It was a quiet affair. Mrs. Teasdale fainted and had to be helped away.'

'I bet she did! Trust Elvira. Ever since she was a nipper she's made a drama out of every event in life. Hysterics when her mother died; had a fit at the graveside when they buried her. I often wondered what happened on her honeymoon. I'll bet Lady Macbeth wasn't in it!'

He paused, gasping for breath, but he looked a bit better. Excitement had brought back some of his colour.

'I'd better attend to the fire, sir.'

Littlejohn went through the previous ritual again. He carried in a shovelful of coal from the tumbledown coal-shed, filled up the scuttle with cobs, threw some pieces of wood on the embers in the grate to coax them into flames.

'Help yourself to a drink…'

'Not just now, sir.'

'That's serious. Help me to one, then.'

Littlejohn gave him a whisky and soda.

'Well, what do you want? I don't flatter meself you've called to ask about my health or to fill up the fire. What is it this time?'

'I want to know what happened to Ryder, sir.'

'How the hell should I know? He's just done a bunk. I haven't checked the silver or the ready cash. Don't feel up to it, but I'll bet something's missin'.'

'I don't believe he left Basilden, sir. I'd be surprised if he even got far from this house.'

Scott-Harris scuffled with his shawls and sat up. He groaned like somebody hurt as he levered himself half upright.

'You're not hintin' that I might have something to do with his vanishin'!'

'First of all, sir, don't you think you ought to call in the doctor? You look in very poor shape. I'd think all the happenings of the past few days have been too much for you...'

'Blast it, man, get on with what you've got to say! I don't need a doctor. I can look after myself. A day or so's rest and I'll be as fit as a fiddle. Must have caught a cold or somethin'.'

'Well, I think you ought to have the doctor, just the same. However... I've called to ask you what happened last Sunday night after Mr. Teasdale and his wife called.'

Scott-Harris grunted, took a swig of his whisky, and sank down on the couch again.

'I'll bet any money, you know already. Somebody among all that lot, not exceptin' my family, would be only too glad to tell you. So why bother me?'

'I want your description of what went on. Why did you send for Harry Wood?'

'That's an easy one. I sent for him because Elvira wouldn't believe that Jimmy was running a show on the fair and keepin' another woman.'

'You told her before Sunday?'

'Of course I did. I wouldn't put it past her to tell you I didn't. You've been questioning her, haven't you?'

'Yes.'

'And I'll wager she gave you a dramatic recital about it, too, didn't she? Yes, I told her and she said it was a lie. You see, she couldn't believe that such a thing could happen to her. An adulterous husband runnin' a hoop-la stall on a fairground. She refused to believe it. Her pride wouldn't let her. When it comes to pride, Elvira's an ostrich. Head in the sand.'

'So you confronted her with Harry Wood. Ryder, I assume, told you, in the first place.'

'Yes. And I told Elvira. So, as she wouldn't believe it second-hand, I made up my mind she should have it straight from the horse's mouth.'

'Did Ryder try blackmail in connection with this information he'd come by?'

'He hinted. But he'd got hold of the wrong chap when he mentioned it to me. Tell it, and be damned, I told him.'

'Had he tried it on Teasdale, too?'

'Yes. Why?'

'Because, just before his death, Ryder was flush with money. He'd a pocketbook full of notes.'

'For some reason... and mind you, it wasn't his family he was thinkin' of... For some reason Jimmy didn't want it to get out...'

'He promised the other woman in the case he wouldn't ask for a divorce until later. You see she happened to be a decent sort and didn't want him to bring disgrace on his family. He'd made up his mind to ask for a divorce sooner or later, but he also was intent on keeping his promise to the woman.'

'So he paid Ryder to shut up. However, after it all came out last Sunday, Teasdale pitched into Ryder and threatened to tell the police.'

'What evidence of blackmail could Teasdale have given to the police?'

'I think he'd paid up to Ryder the previous time he was back here. A week last Sunday. In the course of a row he had here with Ryder on Sunday night, he said he'd still got the note Ryder sent him giving instructions where they'd meet for the handover. He said the police would soon recognise the writing. That shook Ryder. I don't suppose the evidence was conclusive, but if it had been, it might have seen Ryder off for quite a stretch. You see, he'd previous convictions, and a charge of blackmail, well...? Would you say five years?'

There was a large steel engraving on the wall opposite the fire and, beneath it, a cavalry sabre in its sheath, hanging from a hook. Littlejohn went across the room and took it from the wall.

'Leave that alone. I like your damn' cheek. Put it back.'

Littlejohn withdrew the sabre from the sheath. It was clean and bright.

'I hear you chased Teasdale round the room with this last Sunday, sir.'

He snapped the blade back and hung the weapon in its place again.

'Elvira told you that, too, eh? I can imagine her. Real melodrama, eh? Outraged father pursuing betrayer of his daughter with drawn sword. Right up Elvira's street that. Did you believe her?'

'Yes, until you can prove otherwise. But first of all, let's begin where you faced Teasdale and his wife with Harry Wood. You accused Teasdale to his face about his double life and then trotted in Harry to confirm it.'

'That's right. As I said, Elvira wouldn't take my bare word. So…'

'What did Teasdale say to that?'

'Lost his silly little temper. Hit Wood across the face. Just like him. Slapped him, instead of punchin' him on the jaw like a man. Me and Ryder had to interfere and stop him. I think he'd have strangled Harry Wood. Wood was twice as big, and heavy, but he's yellow-livered and was scared. Instead of hittin' him back, he backed away. Ryder told him he'd better go before Jimmy killed him, and the cowardly blighter went hot-foot.'

Littlejohn was watching Scott-Harris closely. He spoke to him casually. 'And then when Wood had gone, Teasdale turned on you, sir.'

Scott-Harris said nothing at first. He stared at him with a frown on his forehead, his eyes popping. His thoughts were wandering and he seemed to be making a tremendous effort to follow what was being said.

'How much do you really know, Littlejohn? I'd almost say you were here when it happened. Did Elvira tell you, or was it that swine Ryder?'

'Never mind that. Teasdale turned on you, then. He called you all the names he could lay his tongue to.'

The old man hardly moved a muscle. He was too taken aback even to speak.

'He said he wanted a divorce and abused you some more. Finally, you said you'd kill him for all he'd said and done. You then took down the sabre from the wall, and he laughed at you for your pains. Then Teasdale set about Ryder and his blackmail.'

'That's it! That's right! I only took the sword to frighten him and make him eat humble pie. The silly little pipsqueak. To threaten and abuse me. Me! When he found out he couldn't upset me, he tried it on Ryder. Shook Ryder, too, by gad!'

'He was then going to make an exit after leaving Ryder to stew, but you called him back.'

Scott-Harris sat up. He panted and wheezed and groped for his glass again.

'Pour me another.'

He guzzled down half the whisky in a gulp.

'You're right. I sent Elvira out of the room. I was goin' to make Teasdale sit up for his cheek. He'd cursed me and tried to make me look small. I'd no intention of doin' the same in the presence of a woman. So I sent her out. I was goin' to show Jimmie that when it came to cursing, he was just an amateur. I was going to make him crawl.'

'So, in the absence of your daughter, you and Ryder set about Teasdale and beat him up. Is that right?'

Scott-Harris hadn't foreseen that. He pawed the air and although half lying on the couch, he seemed to lose his balance, clutched at the table beside him, and sent the bottles and glasses crashing to the floor.

'Major Scott-Harris! Pull yourself together.'

It didn't calm the old man. He thrashed about, livid now.

'So, Elvira told you that, did she? She's a damned liar. I just told him off and showed him the door, and he went. Now, let's get this straight, once and for all, Littlejohn. She's told you a tale so that you'll come here and enrage me. Or, you might even arrest me. She knows my blood pressure's in a dangerous state and my heart's dicky. She hopes you'll upset me so much that it'll kill me. Or maybe she wishes you'd arrest me as murderer of Jimmie, and hang me. It's diabolical... It's... It's...'

His eyes were jutting from his head. He looked almost raving mad. Then, suddenly, he quietened off. He lay back on the couch gasping.

'Let me tell you somethin', Littlejohn. Elvira hates me. Shall I tell you why? Money. She's always wanted me out of the way. Her mother's money comes to her then. The other two sisters are the same, but they're not highly strung and unbalanced like Elvira and they act more discreetly and keep quiet about it. But they think the same. They want to see the last of me. The income on my late wife's estate comes to me for life and when I die, the capital's divided among the three of 'em. Thirty thousand pounds or thereabouts, nominal. No wonder they want me to die. A stroke, a heart attack, or even hangin'. It's all the same to them. They expect ten thousand apiece! Quite a windfall after the life the three of 'em have led, mere existences with a trio of husbands who're nonentities... penniless nincompoops. But they're in for a shock. I said thirty thousand nominal. Most of the money is in War Loan bought at 104. Now it's at 57, making the cash capital about £16,000. A little over five thousand apiece!'

Littlejohn sat quietly in the chair beside the couch. Then he slowly bent down, picked up the bottles and set the table right. He spoke casually again.

'What happened to Teasdale?'

'He left like a whipped dog after I'd finished with him.'

'Are you sure?'

'You'll have to take my word for it.'

'What was all the commotion that occurred after your daughter left you and Ryder with him and went in the next room?'

'So, you're still harpin' on that. I told you she's a liar. She wants me to be accused of murder. Well, I didn't kill Teasdale. I tell you, I didn't.'

'I'm not saying you did. But what happened? Why did Ryder go in the street and drive Teasdale's car to the back of the house?'

'I don't know what you're talking about.'

'I think you do, sir. Why should Ryder move the car if Teasdale went away through the front door on his own two feet?'

'Your guess is as good as mine. I didn't know the car had been moved.'

He sank back again, limp, a dead weight. There wasn't a sound, except the ticking of the clock and the hiss of the coals in the grate.

'What happened to Ryder?'

The old man groaned as though in pain again.

'I tell you, I don't know. Why keep on askin' the same silly questions? Go and ask those who've told you all the other rubbish. As far as I know, things must have got too hot for him, and he bolted into hiding. I don't know where he's gone.'

'Ryder isn't hiding. He's dead.'

More scuffling among the shawls and Scott-Harris sat up on the couch again.

'How do you know?'

'If he hadn't been, we'd have laid him by the heels by now. Half the police in the country are after him. He'd have shown up somewhere if he'd been alive.'

'Well, I can't help you. I don't know a thing about it. He went to bed one night; in the morning he'd gone.'

'The night I was here and saw him coming home?'

'It might have been. I'm too tired to remember...'

He waved his hand about limply. His eyes were bloodshot and his thin remaining hair was dishevelled and sticking out from the back of his head.

'Look here. I've had enough. I'm not well. You'd better leave me. As you say, I'd do with a doctor. I've told you all I know and if I send for Dr. Macallister, he'll stop you from this pesterin'. You'd better ring him up.'

'Very well, sir. What's his number?'

'It's in the book on the table by the 'phone there.'

Littlejohn rang up the doctor. A woman answered. He had been called out to Cassons' Mill. Two firemen had been injured and a number of operatives, caught in an upper room, had been burned. The doctor would call at Rangoon as soon as possible.

'The doctor's been called out to a fire at Cassons' Mill, sir. He'll come round as soon as he gets in. Meanwhile you'd better take a rest and don't excite yourself any more...'

Littlejohn straightened the rugs and the shawl and made the old man comfortable. Scott-Harris was looking washed out again now, the same palour and swelled purple veins which Littlejohn had seen when first he called.

'Before I go, sir, I'd just like to take a look over the house to make sure that there's no trace of Ryder or that he's not taken anything away with him. Besides, we may get a clue as to his whereabouts.'

Scott-Harris reared up again, too exhausted to sit straight, resting with his face on his hand, propped up on his elbow.

'Damn' cheek! Search the place, did you say? I won't allow it.'

Littlejohn sighed. Nothing but trouble and frustration where the major was concerned.

'I'm sorry, sir. I thought you mightn't object. My colleague will soon be here with a search warrant and...'

Scott-Harris sat upright, dangling his swollen feet in their red leather slippers, clutching the couch to hold himself erect.

'Search warrant? It's a scandal. Why search my place? I didn't kill Teasdale. As for Ryder, go and search the town and where he's known, instead of upsettin' me and my home.'

'We applied for the warrant because you won't co-operate, sir. From the very beginning, you've made it difficult for us. We must find Ryder. You understand. We've got to find Ryder.'

Scott-Harris cooled off. He even gave Littlejohn a look of reproach. There was something crafty in the look, too, but Littlejohn couldn't guess what it was about.

'Don't get excited, then, Littlejohn. Nothin' to get excited about. I've nothin' to hide. Search the damned house, if you want. Ground floor to attics. All the same to me. You won't find Ryder. I tell you, he bolted from here. It must have got too hot for him.'

'Very well, sir. Lie down again, then, and don't be upset. I won't disturb anything.'

The major settled down and Littlejohn left him, the door open in case he called for anything.

There were attics. He climbed to them first. Dusty and forlorn places, once occupied by servants. There were still iron bedsteads in two of them, with soiled straw mattresses. The rest, mere junk. Old furniture, hip-baths, boxes, trunks, piles of books and magazines. The third attic must have been a playroom when the girls were young. There was an ancient rocking-horse, which still moved rhythmically to and fro as Littlejohn instinctively pushed it. And a soiled doll's house, some old skittles, a couple of cracked rubber balls with their colour worn away. Finally, a row of dolls, three of them, staring into space, dressed in moth-eaten little frocks. It all looked as if, suddenly, when the nursery was alive and the girls at play, someone had entered and carried them away, never to return.

The floor below had four bedrooms, a boxroom and an old-fashioned bathroom. Littlejohn entered them all, one by one. Ryder's quarters he had visited before. Then, two bedrooms containing old wooden beds and bedroom suites. The mattresses, soiled like the others on the floor above, were there, dusty, moth-eaten. The smell of damp, decay, and that stony, dry-rotten odour of old houses and neglected rooms hung about. Finally, Scott-Harris's bedroom, larger and packed with old furniture, on the front of the house. It was tidy, the bed was made, but there was dust on the chairs, dressing-table and desk. Dust which had not been disturbed for days by human intrusion. It looked as if, since Sunday last, at least, Scott-Harris had not been upstairs, never slept in the great double bed, which he had once occupied with his sad-looking wife, never even opened the flat half-bottle of brandy lying on its side on the table by the bed.

Littlejohn looked around. No point in opening drawers, in searching here and there for evidence. He wanted Ryder, at present, and nothing else. And Ryder and all his possessions had vanished as though he had never lived in the house at all.

His eye caught a drawer open a mere half-inch, clumsily closed by whoever had handled it last, held open by a small wedge of cotton-wool escaping from the inside. He pulled it and looked in.

It was used for first-aid equipment. Lint, cotton-wool, surgical gauze, bottles of iodine, aspirin, bromide. Surgical scissors, tweezers... He didn't touch any of them. He noticed that the cotton-wool and the lint packets had been hastily torn open and part of the contents plucked from their places by rough hands, too busy, too eager even to straighten the paper again, but merely to thrust the remainder back and not even close it properly in the drawer.

He had looked over all the upper floors and found nothing to throw any light on Ryder's disappearance. There were, of course, the cotton-wool and the lint, both rifled from large packets. They suggested to his mind the packing of a wound to stop it from bleeding and leaving traces wherever the body was hastily carried, and perhaps in the car which was bearing it away for disposal. He slowly descended the stairs.

There was still no sign of Cromwell or Naizbitt. He opened the front door and looked out. It was now quite dark. In the sky ahead, a bright glow and the reflection of flames flickering on the clouds banked in the east.

In the rooms above, he had needed to switch on the lights as he went along, revealing dusty globes, fittings festooned with cobwebs. Now, he turned on the hall light and all those on his way to the other rooms and rear quarters. Scott-Harris was lying in the dark, with only the glow of the fire for illumination.

It was the same downstairs. The neglected morning-room where Elvira Teasdale had been sent to wait whilst Scott-Harris and Ryder dealt with her husband. Then, the main dining-room, unused, too, with a long double-pedestal table, at which six chairs were still spread, as though guests might at any time arrive for a dusty dinner. The place was cold and smelled of earth.

The kitchens. Nobody had done much there since Ryder's disappearance. Dishes were piled up in the large sinks, the pots and pans untouched, apparently, since the manservant had last gathered them in an untidy mass on the large table ready for washing-up. In the larder, a half pork-pie was growing mould and a camembert cheese had liquified into a sticky mess which stank to high heaven.

There was nothing more to investigate, nothing worth obtaining a search warrant to cover, indoors, at least. What the dank garden and rotting outhouses would reveal was another matter and would have to wait.

Then he came to the last door to be opened. It was locked. It stood beneath the wide staircase and was obviously the way to the cellars. Littlejohn returned to the sitting-room and switched on the light.

'Excuse me, sir. Hope I'm not disturbing you.'

Scott-Harris was lying quietly under his rugs. He grunted to clear his throat.

'Seen all you want to see? Not much use for a search warrant, had you? Well, I suppose you'll be goin' on your way, now. Time one of my grand-daughters called to find me some food and tidy up a bit. That is, if they can spare the time from chasing young fellahs all over the town...'

'I've not been in the cellars, sir. The door's locked... the one under the stairs.'

Silence for a moment.

'Just tryin' to think what we've got in 'em, now. They're so damned dark and we haven't electric light down there. They're damp and empty. Not much use to you, Superintendent.'

'All the same, sir, I think I'd better finish the job properly.'

'Can't you take my word for anythin'? I tell you they're...'

'May I have the key, sir?'

'I don't know where it is. Haven't been down there for years.'

'When my colleagues arrive with the warrant, then, we'll have to break it in.'

'Smash the lock, then, and be damned to you!'

'Very well, sir.'

Littlejohn made for the door.

Scott-Harris still didn't move, but spoke from the mass of rugs.

'Might find it behind the larder door. That's where it used to be kept.'

Then another silence.

The key was in its place. Large and old, but obviously recently used. Perhaps by Ryder.

He unlocked the door and looked down the steep wooden stairs. It was as black as the pit below. Nothing to see, except the stairs disappearing in the void.

Littlejohn was without his torch and took out his petrol-lighter. A couple of flicks and the wick was alight. He stood on the top step looking down, seeing nothing by the small flickering flame. A draught blew up the stairs and extinguished it. He turned towards the light shining in from the hall. He was just in time.

Standing on the top step, his arms outstretched like some huge animal, was Scott-Harris, and, as Littlejohn turned, the major tottered and then launched himself upon him. Illuminated by the light behind, the old man looked huge, monstrous, a shaking mountain of flesh, which, as Littlejohn braced himself to resist it, engulfed him. The heaving body seemed to flow over him, quivering like a nightmare slug or a mass of jelly. He clung to it desperately, but the hands moved about his arms, seeking out his fingers, clamping themselves upon them, gripping them like vices and struggling to tear them away and cast him down into the darkness.

Littlejohn sought with his feet for something against which to brace himself in the uneven struggle and his heel contacted the upright beam from which the staircase was hung. He flexed his leg and then with all his strength straightened it. At the same time, he thrust against the mass of flesh with one free hand. He felt the body of the fat man suddenly relax and reel. With a wild cry, like that of a wounded animal, Scott-Harris collapsed backwards, flattened out on the floor, and lay still.

Littlejohn could not take the single step upwards to reach the lighted hall. He was completely exhausted, breathless, and his knees trembled with fear. Sweat seemed to pour from every part of his body and streamed down his face until he could taste the salt of it in his mouth.

Slowly he pulled himself together and dragged himself to the landing and into the light.

Scott-Harris was lying flat on his back in the doorway. He was still alive and his breath came in long snores, as though he were gulping in more and more air to prevent his body from dying.

The old man was wearing a shabby suit and Littlejohn loosed his collar and thrust his hand down the top of the camel-hair waistcoat to feel for the heart. He quickly withdrew it.

His hand was covered in blood.

16

THE NEW MASTER

CROMWELL, NAIZBITT AND THE DOCTOR ARRIVED TOGETHER, by which time Littlejohn had, by dragging and hoisting, laid the huge form of Major Scott-Harris on the couch. He had stripped and examined the wound, a deep stab beneath the left collar-bone. Scott-Harris had apparently tried to treat his injury himself without much success, for it was now badly infected and needed prompt and skilled attention.

This explained his rummaging in the first-aid drawer upstairs and his weak condition over the past few days. How the wound had been inflicted, Scott-Harris alone could explain.

When he saw Cromwell, Littlejohn forgot momentarily Scott-Harris and the case, for his sergeant had bandaged hands and bedraggled clothes, in spite of which he had insisted on reporting as soon as the doctor had treated him. His bowler hat was set grimly above his sooty face and he gave Littlejohn an apologetic look for his late arrival.

Naizbitt explained. John Casson had just signed the search warrant in his smoke-filled office, when the boardroom next door had suddenly burst into flames as the sparks blown from the adjacent mill had fired the heavy curtains. In no time, the place had become a mass of fire. Casson's setter-dog had been in the room and Casson himself had dashed through the flames to release the trapped animal, only to fall, overcome by smoke and fumes. Then Cromwell had rescued the pair of them. He later received official commendation for his courage.

The doctor attended to Scott-Harris right away.

'I wonder how this happened. It's a stab wound from a knife. Another inch or so and it would have penetrated the lung and heart. And it's a day or two old, too.'

Littlejohn shook his head.

'Don't ask me, doctor. I can only guess.'

'It looks as if he's been trying to dress it himself. It's infected and suppurating badly. We'd better get him to hospital right away. I'll ring for an ambulance. I've put a temporary dressing on it.'

'He must have been afraid to send for medical help in case the whole story came out.'

'What story?'

Littlejohn left the room, after restraining Cromwell, who rose to follow him. He gently pushed him back in his chair.

'Just rest, old chap. You're all in. I'll be back in a minute. Lend me your torch if you've got it.'

Cromwell passed over his small pocket lamp. He was rarely caught unprepared.

The light bobbed its way down the cellar steps as Littlejohn descended.

The foot of the stairs was a shambles.

A heap of clothing, with coat-hangers protruding, clean and dirty linen, two suitcases, and all Ryder's personal belongings down to his toothbrush, apparently flung headlong into the depths. The old man must have gathered the lot in his arms and thrown them down from the top.

Under the motley pile, the body of Ryder, cold and stiff. He lay on his back, his arms and legs spreadeagled, his neck broken. But for a stroke of luck, Littlejohn might have ended in the same way when Scott-Harris attacked him. He could imagine the manservant struggling in vain against the huge mass of relentless flesh, pushed by the human steam-roller to the top of the steps and then, after a frantic effort to save himself, hurling backwards into space and down on the stone floor below.

Littlejohn flashed the torch round the squalid interior of the cellar. Old parcels, packing cases, trunks, timber, broken furniture, two tumbledown women's bicycles. Some bottles of wine in dusty bins. The whole place smelled of drains and rotten wood. A shining object on the floor almost a yard from Ryder's body, reflected the light from the torch. It was a small, sharp-pointed game-carver, perhaps the first weapon to his hand, with which Ryder had tried to defend himself and which must have catapulted from his grip as he fell to his death.

Littlejohn slowly made his way back up the stairs. He turned as he reached the top and surveyed for a moment the wreckage at the bottom. The old man had temporarily hidden the body and all Ryder's belongings in the darkness, but, weakened by his wound and perhaps the violence of his victim, he had been quite incapable of doing anything more to conceal permanently the damning evidence of his crime.

Scott-Harris was still on the couch, groaning now.

'I want Littlejohn. I want to speak to him. I've things to say to him before the ambulance comes. The rest of you may as well hear it, too.'

He paused, wheezing and short of breath. He could hardly speak or collect his thoughts.

'You're in no condition to talk, Major. You can tell the Superintendent anything you like when you're stronger.'

Opposition stimulated Scott-Harris. He roared feebly.

'Dammit, man, I'm goin' to talk to him before I leave this place and nobody's going to stop me.'

He stretched out a puffy hand at Littlejohn.

'Come here...'

'Give me a drink first…'

The doctor helped him to a small brandy. It seemed to do him good, but he said it wasn't enough. The doctor didn't seem to hear his complaint.

'I didn't intend to kill him. I suppose you've found him. It was self-defence. Remember. Make a note of that. Self-defence. The swine came at me with a knife. So, I pushed him down the cellar steps.'

'Just as you tried to do to me, sir?'

'I'm sorry about that, Littlejohn. You've been damned decent to me. But I got in a panic. Knew what you'd find at the bottom, you see.'

'Who killed Teasdale?'

'Ryder. I might as well tell you, there was no question of him blackmailing Teasdale. I made it up. I gave Ryder two hundred pounds in cash to get rid of the body. When Elvira went out, I started to tell Jimmie off, but he grew violent, the little devil. Actually punched me on the jaw because I called that woman of his by a good old English name. Ryder tried to restrain him. Teasdale seemed to see red. He told Ryder he'd caused all this by blowing the gaff on him about Wood seeing him at Lowestoft Fair. Got hold of Ryder by the throat. He was like a madman. Shook Ryder like a terrier with a rat. I thought he'd kill him. Ryder clawed down a small dirk that used to hang over there…'

He pointed between his feet to a spot on the wall. There was only a mere nail protruding there now.

'Ryder stabbed him in the back before I could stop him. He later took the knife with the scabbard and hid it somewhere. I don't know where. Teasdale didn't even cry out. Just dropped dead. We were in a fix, I can tell you.'

Scott-Harris stopped and gasped for breath. The doctor protested.

'Leave me alone. Where was I? Jimmie dropped dead. And then, damn it, if Elvira didn't walk in. Ryder had disentangled himself from the body and was standin' with me, both dumbfounded by it, and when she saw Teasdale with the knife in his back, she turned on *me*. "So you kept your promise and killed him?" And that swine Ryder told her it *was* me. I'd no proof otherwise, and she believed Ryder because of what I'd said I'd do when I was in a temper.'

He paused, exhausted again, hardly able to make himself heard.

'Give me some more brandy.'

The doctor gave him another spoonful and then waited no longer, but dialled and called an ambulance.

'I'm not goin' till I've finished. As I was saying, Ryder saw his chance and played up to Elvira. She honestly thought I'd done it. I couldn't convince her. "I won't tell, Daddy," she said, but I knew she would. Like when she was a little girl. Drove me mad with her lying. She kept away when you were here, afraid of what I'd do and say. There was no time to argue. What were we goin' to do with the body? Elvira was as cool as a blasted cucumber. She said we ought to send it to *that woman* of Jimmie's. That gave Ryder an idea. He found out where Jimmie was due to go from Basilden. A place called Tylecote, not far from Ely. Ryder took the body there through the night and dumped it in the river. We all thought they'd think either the woman or some enemy of Teasdale's on the fairground had done it. Never think of suspectin' he'd been killed here. Well, it seems we were wrong. One day you must tell me why and how we slipped up.'

Scott-Harris seemed to recover a bit through indignation. He tugged at the front of Littlejohn's coat.

'Ryder had a hell of a journey through floods and darkness. He ditched Jimmie's old car and came back by train. And what do you think he said when he got back here next mornin', eh? "My bill will be a couple of hundred quid for that job. On account." Mind you, when I paid it, I told him plainly that it wasn't blackmail. Just appreciation of what he'd done and been through. Know what he said then? "You've got a new lodger, Major. I'm moving to better accommodation to-morrow and I wouldn't be surprised if I didn't want the best bedroom one day." When he heard you'd arrived he also threatened to tell you what happened if I didn't treat him right. "Your daughter will confirm that, too. She's up to the neck in it and she knows her own father killed Teasdale in a fit of temper."'

Littlejohn nodded.

'By the way, Major, you found the two hundred pounds in Teasdale's pocket, didn't you? He'd brought it with him, perhaps with the idea of buying off Ryder, but he changed his mind.'

'I only borrowed the money. I swear I'd have paid it back to Elvira.'

The doctor, impatient to get Scott-Harris to the hospital, kept looking reproachfully first at Littlejohn and then at the other two policemen. The old man on the couch seemed almost in a state of collapse. He closed his eyes and moaned to himself.

'He's been drinking heavily and that on top of the shock he's had and the wound...'

'He'll pull through all right, doctor?'

'I can't say until I've examined him properly.'

'Could you give him a brief once-over? You see, I don't want to question him too much now, if it will upset him more. That can come later if he'll recover.'

'I suppose I could. Just until the ambulance arrives...'

He hurried out to his car and returned with his bag from which he took out a sphygmomanometer for taking blood pressure. Then he gently withdrew the old man's arm from under the shawls and started to fix the apparatus.

Scott-Harris opened his eyes.

'What the hell are you doing now?'

'A little examination. It won't inconvenience you. Just relax.'

The doctor carefully set about his task. He couldn't believe the first result and took the reading twice again. Then he listened to the heart through his stethoscope.

'H'm.'

The ambulance arrived at the gate. Passers-by stopped and formed a little inquisitive knot at the front. The two uniformed men emerged and dragged out a stretcher.

During the commotion of their entry, the doctor whispered to Littlejohn.

'The blood pressure's absolutely terrifying. As for the heart, it's enlarged and nearly worn out. He might pop off any time.'

'Is there a chance?'

'He wants a long rest and skilled attention. Might live for years in the right circumstances. One thing's imperative. No more alcohol.'

'You'd better tell him that at an appropriate time.'

The ambulance men were standing waiting to carry the old man off, but he wasn't ready.

'I've not done yet. Want to get everything off my chest and then I can either have a good rest in the hospital or else just die. I'm not going till I've finished.'

Littlejohn raised his eyebrows at the doctor.

'Very well. Better let him finish it. If we don't, he'll probably try to resist or else natter himself into a stroke or a heart attack. I'll give him an injection.'

Scott-Harris must have been listening.

'A tot of brandy'll do more good.'

'No. Now just keep quiet a minute and then you can go on talking. But take it easy and make it short. You ought to be in bed, you know.'

The old man swore as the needle penetrated. He must have felt it a bit undignified to be manhandled.

'Come here, Littlejohn. Don't keep messin' about the room when I want to talk to you.'

Littlejohn drew up a chair and sat beside the couch.

'Where was I?'

'You said Ryder talked about moving into the best bedroom.'

The ambulance men looked on wide-eyed. They hadn't expected this. Now and then they officiated at a death-bed scene or a confession. But a murderer telling how he did it! This was something worth listening to. They strained to catch every word.

The mention of Ryder's impudence revived Scott-Harris. He raised himself on his elbow, his chest heaving, his eyes savage.

'Yes. It wasn't till I was alone that the full meanin' of what Ryder said dawned on me. He thought he'd got me properly in his clutches and was goin' to levy blackmail till he was the master and I was the servant. I had to think a way out. I couldn't tolerate that, At first, I thought I'd better see my solicitor and if necessary, go to the police. On Tuesday night, Ryder came in the room and started to set the table for a meal. He laid two places...'

Scott-Harris's lips trembled and he gasped for breath.

'I told him to damn' well unlay one of them. He just smiled and did nothin'. So I gathered up the extra cups, plates, and the rest and chucked 'em in the hearth. Do you know what he said? "That'll cost you another hundred quid, Major. I don't take any more domineering from you. You've got to pay up for it, or else take the consequences."'

He turned to Littlejohn a bit pathetically.

'I'm a hot-tempered man, Littlejohn. Can't help it. It's my nature. I just took hold of Ryder by the throat and shook him till his damned false teeth rattled. I couldn't let the little rat go; I wanted to choke him. There was a cold pie on the table with a small carver beside it. Ryder struggled a bit and then took up the knife and struck me. I felt the blade enter my chest, but I had no pain at the time. The blood spurted out and that maddened me more. I held him by both arms and forced him into the hall. I really don't know yet why I did that. He still had the knife and was trying to stab me again. I can see his silly little frightened face full of panic and wild with fear. He thought his last minute had come. I guess it was just the route our struggles took us... Out into the hall, and there I saw the cellar door open. Ryder must have been down. I keep some port there and I could smell it on his breath as we fought. He'd been celebratin'.'

He looked at the circle of faces round him.

'I don't mind you all listenin'. It makes no difference now. Where's the doctor?'

The doctor, a tall Scotsman with a long rugged face, turned from examining one of the large pictures on the wall, a still-life with pheasants surrounded by tomatoes and onions.

'I'm here, Major.'

'I've nearly finished. Sorry to keep you like this, but I must get it off my chest in case I don't come through.'

Unusually polite for Scott-Harris, but then the whole affair was unusual. You didn't know what was coming next.

'The open cellar door... That's what I was sayin', wasn't it? Well, I just pushed him along, gripping his two arms to keep the knife away and chucked him down the cellar steps. I heard him hit the bottom and then it all went quiet. I felt too ill to go down and see what had happened. I'd never have got back up the stairs again. I just locked the door. Since then, I've looked down with a light. He's still there, just as he was when he fell. He's dead.'

Littlejohn could see it all again. The little blackmailer giving the major enough punishment to kill a normal man, but the great corpulent balloon resisted, surrounded him, rendered him helpless, and flung him into the darkness. He stood up and bent over the old man. He couldn't help the compassion in his voice as he spoke.

'And you cleared out his room and threw all his things on top of him. It made it seem as if he'd run away, didn't it?'

'That's right. I had in mind buryin' the body and the rest somewhere in the garden later, but my strength went gradually and I'd not enough energy to do it. That's all.'

Scott-Harris allowed Littlejohn to push him gently back on the couch. He seemed quite sober now. He was all in, a poor old thing with swollen legs and a body almost like an elephant.

Steps along the path, and suddenly Elvira entered. She came in, panting, halted in the middle of the room, gave a dazed look round, and then put her hand dramatically over her heart.

'They said the ambulance had come to take Father away...'

Her eyes were fixed on the couch.

'Father!'

But she didn't approach any nearer. She seemed held back by something, probably fear.

'What is it?' she asked the doctor.

Nobody answered.

The grandfather clock ticked on, the two ambulance men looked at one another and seemed inspired by the same thought. They'd no business there. They tiptoed out. The shoes of one of them squeaked and seemed to make a fearful row in the silence.

Elvira remained in the middle of the room, her hands gripping her bag. She didn't know what to say.

It was all over. The case had worked itself out. The only thing to do now was to wait. The puzzle had fallen into shape. Elvira waiting for the money her mother had left tied up during Scott-Harris's lifetime. The three girls, Elvira, Phoebe and Chloe, hoping the old man would soon die. And Elvira suddenly faced with a chance to speed his end.

The major slowly opened his eyes and saw her.

'Oh, it's you, is it? A nice mess you've landed me in. Why didn't you tell the truth, instead of taking Ryder's part. You knew I'd never have murdered Jimmy.'

Littlejohn gently pushed him down again.

'Don't excite yourself, sir. You'll make yourself ill.'

'Leave me alone, Littlejohn. I'm speakin' to Elvira. Listen. You think the old chap's goin' to snuff it, don't you? Well, I'm not. I'll be a model patient when I get to the hospital. I'll do all they tell me, and more. I'm goin' to live to eighty, or even ninety, just for the pleasure of seein' you poor and needin' money. When the girls are married, you'll be alone, and you'll have no Jimmie bringin' in the money from his hoop-la. You'll have to come beggin' to me...'

He shouted it in a hoarse voice. Then he sank back and closed his eyes. He seemed to be smiling to himself as though he were enjoying a good joke.

'You can come and live here then and take Ryder's job. Look after your old dad. It'll brighten the place up to have some young blood about.'

He said it with his eyes closed and actually laughed.

'I'm ready, doctor.'

The ambulance men came back and carried him off.

Elvira did not move. Her nostrils had grown pinched and she looked years older. Her face had turned yellow and her eyes had sunk in their dark orbits. Then she fainted.

It provided a bit of relief reviving her. Finally, she sat moaning on the couch.

'Is he badly ill?'

Nobody answered. There were only three of them there now. Littlejohn, Cromwell and Naizbitt. They didn't know how it was going to end.

Littlejohn stood with his hands in his pockets, his pipe in his mouth.

'We'll take you home in the police car…'

She looked up at him, fear in her face.

'You knew Ryder killed your husband?'

'I didn't know. I thought it was Father. He said he'd kill him.'

'But you didn't give your father the benefit of the doubt.'

'Ryder said Father did it…'

'Knowing Ryder, how could you believe him against your father's word?'

'I… I…'

'Let's go.'

Major Scott-Harris took a long time to recover, but he kept his word. He was a model patient and in the end, it looked as if he'd see eighty, with a bit of looking after. Finally, about six months after the crimes, he appeared in court on a charge of manslaughter. He was in a wheel-chair, hadn't touched alcohol since admitted to hospital, and put up a good show. A helpless, forsaken old man. The jury sympathised with him and he was acquitted.

Elvira came out of it badly. Her knowledge of her husband's death was against her, but she said to the end that she knew nothing about the disposal of his body. Or of Ryder's death. A plea of mental breakdown arising out of her husband's murder got her off.

During the long wait to the trial, Teasdale's three daughters left home. Irene wed the bookie, Barbara married her doctor and went to live in Edinburgh, and Christine eloped to Canada with the dentist, who had a wife already. Elvira, in spite of her pleading, was left alone in the shop. On her father's return to Rangoon, she followed him, as he'd predicted, to keep house for him. Scott-Harris said when she arrived, that the public trial and airing of the family secrets was his insurance policy. Elvira daren't try to hasten his end; the police had their eyes on her. He's having an easy time, now, with everything done for him. Littlejohn often wonders how long the trio of sisters will have to wait for their inheritance. Elvira, Phoebe and Chloe.

Dear Reader,

We want to tell you about George Bellairs, the forgotten hero of British crime writing.

George Bellairs wrote over fifty novels in his spare time (his day job being a bank manager). They were published by the Thriller Book Club run by Christina Foyle, manager of the world famous Foyle's bookshop, and who became a friend. His books are set at a time when the real-life British Scotland Yard would send their most brilliant of sleuths out to the rest of the country to solve their most insolvable of murders. Bellairs' hero, gruff, pipe-smoking Inspector Littlejohn appears in all of them. Though his world might have moved on, what drove people to murder – jealousies, greed, fear – is what drives them now. George Bellairs' books are timeless.

If you liked this one, why don't you sign up to the George Bellairs mailing list? On signing you will receive exclusive material. From time to time we'll also send you exclusive information and news.

So join us in forming a George Bellairs community. I look forward to hearing from you.

www.georgebellairs.com
George Bellairs Literary Estate

ALSO BY GEORGE BELLAIRS

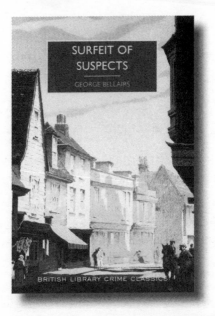

*'At 8 o'clock in the evening on the 8th November,
there was a terrific explosion in Green Lane, Evingden.'*

The offices of the Excelsior Joinery Company have been blown to
smithereens and three of the company directors lie dead amongst the
rubble. When the presence of dynamite is revealed, Superintendent
Littlejohn of Scotland Yard is summoned to the scene.

Beneath the sleepy veneer of Evingden lies a hotbed of deep-rooted
grievances. The new subject of the town's talk, Littlejohn's investigation
is soon confounded by an impressive cast of suspicious persons, each
concealing their own axe to grind.

First published in 1964, Bellairs' novel of small-town grudges with
explosive consequences remains a gripping masterpiece of misdirection.

BRITISH LIBRARY CRIME CLASSICS

Many of our titles are also available in eBook and audio editions